Out of Circulation

A Village Library Mystery, Volume 11

Elizabeth Craig

Published by Elizabeth Spann Craig, 2024.

OUT OF CIRCULATION

First edition. June 18, 2024.

Written by Elizabeth Craig.

Chapter One

L inus gave me a pleading look, silently asking me to intervene. As my favorite library patron, he had good reason to suspect that I'd step in and stop Zelda from being . . . Zelda.

Library volunteer Zelda, naturally, her henna-colored hair fairly bristling, was oblivious and telling Linus exactly what was wrong with him, in great detail.

"You know how much fun you had at trivia night. You gotta be more involved in stuff," she said. "Sitting around and reading all day isn't good for you."

I definitely had to intervene at that point. After all, we were in a public library, and I was a librarian. Besides, Zelda had told me on numerous occasions that she didn't read. Not that she *can't* read, that she doesn't. Which gave me an idea.

I said, "How about if you read a book that Linus suggests every time he joins any sort of activity?"

I was rewarded by a relieved smile from Linus. He pushed his spectacles up his nose, looking anxiously at Zelda to see if she acquiesced.

Zelda's eyes narrowed. "That doesn't sound like a good deal to me. Linus is going to choose a World War II history or some-

1

thing like that. It would take me years to finish it because I'd fall asleep as soon as I started reading. And the activity he joins could be something like the stamp club instead of something that really stretches him."

Linus blinked owlishly behind his glasses. "There's a stamp club?"

Zelda threw up her hands. "See? He's impossible."

"There's some interest in *forming* a philatelist club at the library," I said. "All the details haven't been hammered out yet."

Linus considered this, then cleared his throat. "If we make the rules easy on my end, perhaps we should make them equally generous on Zelda's. How about if *Ann* picks the book?"

Zelda made a face. "It still doesn't sound like a good deal. It'll take me hours and hours to finish a book, like I said. Stamp club is just a single hour."

Zelda was approaching the idea as if I'd asked her to write *I'll read and enjoy a book* two-hundred times on the chalkboard. I shrugged. "This whole deal thing was your idea."

"It wasn't! It was yours!" said Zelda. "I only said Linus needed to stretch himself a little."

Linus, always a gentleman, said, "I appreciate the fact you've been concerned about me. What if we created our own activity until stamp club gets formed? Just the two of us."

Now Zelda's eyes narrowed even more. "What kind of activity? I like stamps about as much as I like books. Meaning not at all."

Linus and I knew exactly how Zelda felt about books. She could have spared us repeating her dislike of them. We winced every time she did. It was a visceral reaction that neither of us seemed to be able to control.

"You do like crosswords, though, right?"

Zelda nodded reluctantly.

"We could try a crossword dual. We'd time ourselves and see how long it takes for us to finish." Linus gestured to the periodicals section of the building, an area he was well-acquainted with, considering he spent long periods of time there every day, always attired in a suit.

"Yeah, but how is that going to work?" demanded Zelda. "There are only so many papers here. You'll work the one in the local paper, and I end up getting stuck with the New York Times puzzle? That doesn't sound fair to me."

I said, "Just take the same paper's puzzle to the copier, copy it, and then set a timer."

Zelda grudgingly considered this. "Okay," she growled. "It's a deal. Let's give it a try after my volunteer shift is over."

She stomped off, as if remembering she *was* on a shift. Linus smiled at me.

"Crisis averted?" I asked.

"Just a temporary reprieve," Linus said wryly, pushing his oversized glasses up his nose again. "But I'll take it." He paused. "Aren't you about to go on vacation? Tomorrow, maybe? I seem to remember that's coming up. Charleston, isn't it?"

"It is. It's a beautiful city. And actually, Grayson and I are heading out this afternoon. I'm leaving work a couple of hours early."

Linus nodded. "I hope you have a calmer vacation than the one you took last time."

Considering the last Charleston vacation involved a couple of murders, I nodded. "Surely, it'll be calmer than that. But we'll be doing different things while Grayson and I are there. My college roommate got engaged, which is one reason I'm taking the vacation time now. We'll be meeting her fiancé, hanging out, all that kind of stuff."

"Maybe you can find some time to spend on the beach, though? In-between events."

I said, "That's a good idea. There's something about the beach that makes life more relaxing. Just lying there in the sun with nothing else to do."

There must have been a wistful note in my voice because Linus smiled sympathetically. My life must seem like total chaos compared to his. "Have you got a good book to read?"

I nodded. "*South of Broad*, by Pat Conroy."

Linus's smile broadened. "Does that even qualify as a beach read? Conroy's books are usually pretty dark."

"You're right, it's probably not light enough to be a beach read. But I wanted to read something set in Charleston by a Charleston writer, and it fit the bill. There's some family tragedy at play in the book, I think."

"Which is right up Conroy's alley. Well, it's sure to be good, at any rate. The man can write." Linus glanced up. "Don't look now, but I think your library director is heading in our direction."

I groaned. It was highly unlikely that Linus was Wilson's intended target. Instead, I had the feeling that Wilson was coming over to saddle me with a project of some sort. He was an excellent manager, but he always seemed to have very little idea of what he'd already put on my plate. And I wondered if he remembered I was about to head out on vacation.

Linus gave me a sympathetic look and shuffled away toward the periodical section. Wilson briskly approached. "Ann, glad you're still here. You're leaving this afternoon for your trip?"

So he did actually remember it. That was a good thing. But now I was wondering what he was trying to have me squeeze in before I left. "That's right."

"Oh good. Excellent, actually." He paused. "Am I right in supposing you'll have some free time during this trip?"

Free time in which I was going to be hopefully trying to relax on the beach with a book. I said, "I'll probably have a little, yes. Although with my friend being engaged, I know we're going out with her new fiancé to dinner and gallery openings and stuff."

"Right, right," said Wilson, although he sounded distracted. I wasn't altogether sure that he'd absorbed the part about my being pretty busy. "Good. I have something I'd love for you to help out with while you're gone. My apologies for not bringing it up until the last minute."

Sadly, this seemed to be Wilson's modus operandi. But I couldn't help but have my curiosity piqued. What library business could he possibly have in Charleston?

He moved us to his office to further discuss whatever he wanted me to do. Now Wilson had an excited look on his face. It was an expression I'd come to know well. When Wilson had a project idea, he was like a dog with a bone. He was definitely someone who came up with big ideas; it was just that he always wanted someone else to implement them.

"I've been looking into local historic preservation," said Wilson.

This didn't really surprise me. Wilson had always had a soft spot for local history, evident in the glass displays we had near the doors. The one that was set up now housed old maps, surveys, and land deeds that documented Whitby's development and expansion over time, along with old photos that showed some of the changes to the town. We also had a small local history room with old newspaper articles and artifacts. But now it sounded as if he might be planning to do something more. Wilson was definitely a big thinker. And oddly, despite all the time he was spending with his girlfriend Mona, he seemed to double-down on the thinking he was doing. I was starting to suspect that he was thinking of library business while he was watching those reality TV shows with Mona.

"Historical preservation sounds like a great idea," I said. I sounded cautious to my own ears. After all, it was likely going to end up being *my* project, at least in some respect. "The library makes sense as a repository for Whitby history."

"There's that part of it, yes. But I was interested in exploring the idea somewhat further. Whitby is a very old town and I'd like the library to partner with the town council to locate and identify areas that should be labeled historic landmarks. You know how interested developers have been in Whitby lately. If we don't move to protect some of our landmarks, they could well end up being bulldozed to make way for shopping centers." Wilson looked indignant at the thought.

I nodded. "Right. What's the best way of finding out which buildings and areas qualify for protection?"

"In one newsletter I subscribe to, a public survey was used in the process. We have a lot of older residents in Whitby who may remember stories from their grandparents. The idea is to tap into that information, back it up with details we locate in the historical archives, and then use it to identify the landmarks."

I said slowly, "How exactly does the survey work?"

Wilson smiled. "That's what I want you to find out. The person who conducted the original survey is Dr. Bianca Donovan. She's the state archaeologist for South Carolina."

I had the sudden feeling that my trip to South Carolina was going to be interrupted by a business call. Or some other type of detour.

Wilson was already prattling on. "It's called a cultural landscape survey. I believe Charleston hired a consultant to design the survey and conduct field research, but I'm certain we can get similar results without having to spend any money."

Wilson was always very protective of the library's funds, and rightfully so. Right now, though, I was less focused on the budget and more focused on how this talk with Dr. Donovan intersected with the trip I was taking that afternoon.

I couldn't get a word in edge-wise, however. Wilson, uncharacteristically, was bubbling about the project and the bubbling was turning him into a much more loquacious person than usual. Ordinarily, our talk would already have been finished. Wilson usually would briefly outline an idea, bark out my mission, then hurry off to his office to brainstorm more work for me to take on. But now we were already *in* his office. And our meeting didn't seem to be wrapping up.

"Historic preservation is one of those areas that sounds a lot dryer than it actually is," he was saying, eyes bright. "Dr. Donovan should have ideas about how to make the survey more interesting to residents, so we can get a stronger response rate. If we don't know what's actually historic in Whitby, we could accidentally develop areas that need to be protected. The library, obviously, would play a smaller role, but we can partner with conservators, the local museum, and civic groups."

He paused to take a breath, and I quickly jumped in. "You're wanting me to call Dr. Donovan? Schedule a video call with her?"

Wilson said, "That was my original thought. But when I contacted her and told her I had a librarian coming down there later today, she suggested you come over and speak with her in person. I think those are always more satisfactory, anyway. It's hard for me to adjust to this wave of video meetings. They don't seem nearly as natural or productive, and they're terrible for networking or developing business relationships. So it's rather nice this will be a face-to-face meeting like we all used to have in the old days."

Which was exactly what I was afraid of. A meeting during my vacation.

Wilson must have finally read my expression. He frowned. "It won't take very long, Ann. I'd say it would be under an hour, surely. She said the consultant had designed a very engaging survey for residents, and I'd like ours to rope in as many people as possible."

I gave him a tight smile. "Got it. I'll need her contact information, of course, so I can schedule a meeting in-between the other things I'll be doing." And the relaxation I'd hoped to find on the beach with my book.

Wilson nodded vaguely, turning to his computer to get the information. "Funny coincidence. Dr. Donovan is the niece of a good friend of mine. Someone I went to school with. He helped me get her phone number." He squinted at his computer screen. "I'll email you her contact details."

I could tell his mind had finally moved on to the other things on his to-do list. I stood up and headed back out to the reference desk. I was accosted on the way by Luna, my coworker and friend. She had a look of consternation on her face and her hands on her hips.

"Did Wilson just ruin your vacation?" she clucked. "Don't tell me. We're short-staffed, and he decided you needed to delay leaving until tomorrow. Or wait. Maybe he gave you a project that's due tonight. That would be another typical Wilson move."

"Actually, you're making me feel slightly better about my meeting with Wilson. Those would be even worse outcomes. No, he just wants me to set up an in-person meeting with a state archaeologist when I'm in Charleston."

"Seriously?" Luna demanded. Her face was red with irritation. Almost as red as the flowing tunic she wore today and the large hoop earrings that matched. Luna had a very free-spirited approach to style, and the kids in the children's department absolutely ate it up. She had the perfect look for a children's librarian. "Wilson couldn't give you the tiniest of breaks? You *never* take vacation days."

"Well, not since the last time I went to Charleston, anyway," I said wryly.

"Yes, but before that, I don't think you've ever taken personal time. What was it this time? A joint project with the Charleston library?"

"No, but don't give him any ideas," I said with a laugh. "He wants to collaborate with some of Whitby's officials and delve into historical preservation. This archaeologist or her consultant apparently came up with some really engaging public survey that he wants her to tell me about. He figured I could have a face-to-face meeting since I'd be down there anyway. Wilson has some sort of personal connection to the woman."

Luna relaxed just a little, although her expression still looked irritated. "Okay. Well, I guess that won't take up too much time. Although you shouldn't even have to think about work while you're away."

I shrugged. "It might be interesting. Who knows? Whitby is a very historic town, so it's not a bad idea to protect various landmarks before developers end up bulldozing them. But yeah, let's hope the meeting is short and that Dr. Donovan isn't the talkative type."

"Fingers crossed. Although I still wish Wilson would just think for a minute."

I said, "How are things with Wilson and your mom?"

Wilson and Mona, Luna's mom, had been dating for a while and were a testament to the fact that opposites do attract. While Mona wasn't quite as free-spirited as Luna, she was still a lot more laid-back, fun-loving, and experimental than Wilson was. For a while, I suspected Wilson even *slept* in his suit and tie, as I'd never seen him without them. In a lot of ways, Wilson and my patron Linus were two peas in a pod.

Luna grinned. "Oh, Mom has to put him in his place from time to time. But mostly? They get along great. There's something about him being so uptight that makes Mom even more soothing than usual. They do really well together." She squinted over at a wall clock. "Speaking of good relationships, I've got Burton and Belle coming by the library in a few minutes."

These were definitely words that I wasn't expecting to hear. Luna and Burton dated for a while, but the relationship hadn't worked out. They were back to being friends now and were both dating other people. For the life of me, though, I couldn't figure out why Burton and his current girlfriend would be coming to the library to see Luna. "You've got me," I said. "Why are they coming by?"

"Storytime," said Luna, clearly enjoying stumping me. "You might not know this, but Belle has a little guy from a previous marriage." Her smug smile grew at my surprised expression.

"I didn't realize that," I said. "All I know about Belle is that Burton met her at Pilates class and that she was a teacher."

"Exactly. It just so happens that today is a teacher's in-service day. Anyway, they're coming over in a few minutes. It should be fun."

Luna's storytimes were always fun. She threw herself totally into the process, using great voices for the characters and puppets to illustrate the story. She was always centering the storytimes around particular themes, like animals, friendship, or different seasons. Sometimes, if there was enough time at the end, she'd have the kids do a small craft they could take home, again on the same theme. The kids always loved it. Actually, I did, too. It was cool to see stories come to life like that.

"Wish I could make it," I said regretfully. "I've got a lot of stuff to wrap up before I leave, though. Especially since I'm leaving work early."

"Don't worry, there will be others. I'm sure summer break will give plenty of opportunities for Belle to come with her little boy." Luna wagged her finger at me. "Don't put in too much work today, Ann. Otherwise, it's going to take too much time to decompress when you leave here."

She was right. I nodded. "Promise. But that library newsletter really does have to be wrapped up. I was just waiting on Wilson to give me the dates for a few of the events."

"Just don't go overboard," said Luna as she headed off to the children's department. "You don't want to have a work hangover on your vacation. If you leave here all stressed out and cramming work in, it's going to take you longer to decompress."

As it happened, I didn't have the chance to go overboard with anything. Zelda created the perfect unexpected distraction. She'd somehow misplaced her reading glasses somewhere in the library. Unable to find them without wearing them, she'd continued with her shelving. By the time I spotted her trying to read the authors' names with her nose practically against the spines of the books, she'd already mistakenly shelved a slew of items. It took some time to both find her glasses (mysteriously in a houseplant by a window) and reshelve the books.

The newsletter, at least, was finished. It was nice not to have anything pressing hanging over my head as I left with Fitz for the day. Even better, I'd done all my packing the night before, so all I needed to do was to fix a snack for Fitz and me, have a little water, and wait for Grayson to pick me up.

And he was right on time. He loved on Fitz as I rolled out my suitcase.

Chapter Two

"All set?" asked Grayson with a smile. He looked at the suitcase. "That's all you're taking?"

I snorted. "Don't get me second-guessing over this stuff. I planned out my outfits for each day, plus a couple of dressier ones in case we end up going out somewhere nice. I have two swimsuits, cat food, and a coverup, among other things. It actually feels like a lot."

"I have the feeling I went overboard," said Grayson, a sheepish grin tugging at his lips. "I ran out of time this morning and ended up frantically throwing clothes together. I always overpack when I do that. But, you know, we need stuff like beach towels for this trip." There was a hint of embarrassment in his voice.

"Yeah, but Holly wouldn't mind if we borrowed those from her. She had half a closet full of beach towels." I didn't add that she might have even more, considering her brother had died not long ago, and she had taken on some of his things, too. Since Grayson was starting to look like he might head back home and repack, I quickly added, "You know, it's better to have too much than too little. You're going to be just fine. If you or I did forget something, it's not like there aren't any stores in Charleston."

"Good point." With that, I coaxed Fitz into his carrier, and we headed out to the car.

"I made some snacks for the road this time, since you put together something amazing for our last car trip," I said.

Grayson perked up. "Did you? That's awesome. I left the office later than I'd planned on and didn't grab a snack." He chuckled. "Apparently, I'm a disaster today."

"You're fine! And thanks for driving. That's a huge load off me today."

We got ourselves settled in the car and Fitz carefully arranged so he had part of a sunbeam in his carrier. Then I pulled out the cinnamon-cranberry oat bars I'd made. Grayson took one gratefully and devoured it before hastily eating another one. "How did everything go at the library today?" he asked.

"Mostly, it was a great day. I got a lot of things done. And, you know, just being at the library makes for a good day, anyway. Zelda managed to create some chaos by losing her reading glasses. You know, the usual."

Grayson glanced over at me, then quickly back at the road. "It sounds like there might be a 'but' there."

"But Wilson, naturally, gave me *more* things to do. One of them while we're on our trip." I shrugged.

"What?" asked Grayson. "He knows this is supposed to be your vacation time."

"Yeah. He doesn't think it's going to take very long. Honestly, it's the kind of thing that *shouldn't* take long. But it still irked me that he gave me an assignment during my time off." I explained to Grayson about the meeting with the state archaeologist and the cultural landscape survey.

Grayson said, "Got it. Okay. Maybe I can help out by digging through the paper's archives."

I said wryly, "That are housed at the library on microfiche."

He grinned at me. "It makes a good excuse to see more of you."

It was a beautiful day and Grayson had the windows cracked and the music playing. Fitz was contentedly napping in his carrier in a sunbeam. We ate our snacks and chatted about our days as we made the trip down there. Four hours later, we were pulling up to Holly's place in downtown Charleston. I loved my little cottage in Whitby, but Holly's house was a close second. It had a generous front porch with a swing, soft rugs over beautiful wood floors, and cheerily painted walls.

Holly came right out, a big smile on her impish face. She had Murphy, her excitable and adorable golden retriever on a leash. "So glad y'all made it!"

Murphy was also glad and made extravagantly happy leaps on us as we came up. Fitz regarded the dog thoughtfully from his carrier, remembering Murphy from the last time. They'd done well together once Murphy had gotten over his initial excitement.

"Look at you!" I said to my old college roommate.

Grayson said, "Engagement definitely suits you." He reached over to give Holly a hug.

I said, "You seem so happy. And look at that ring!"

The ring appeared to be an antique and had both diamonds and sapphires. Holly held her hand out so I could see it close up.

She smiled. "Isn't it pretty? Now come inside! We have tons to catch up on."

Holly helped us unload the car and put everything upstairs in her guest room, chatting all the time. "Daniel took a quick walk, but should be back any minute. Can't wait for you to meet him."

I was curious about meeting Daniel myself. I knew he was a local artist and that Holly was crazy about him, as she should be, considering they were engaged. But it was just about all I knew about him.

Then Grayson and Holly headed back downstairs, Grayson asking a couple of questions about Daniel while I situated Fitz in the guest room. I seemed to have developed a habit of asking Fitz questions and found myself saying, "Do you want me to close the bedroom door so you can get used to things again?"

Maybe the reason I asked the questions is because Fitz always came up with answers. He jumped up on the bed, snuggling into the blanket at the foot of it. Maybe he was ready for a little quiet time after the long car ride. I set up his litter box and water bowl and gently closed the door behind me.

Holly and Grayson had moved to Holly's fenced yard, where Grayson was tossing a tennis ball for an ecstatic Murphy. Holly had brought out a bottle of wine and four glasses, anticipating Daniel's upcoming arrival. Murphy finally stopped bringing the ball back to Grayson, and we settled into patio chairs with our wine.

A few minutes later, Daniel arrived from his walk. He gave us all a lazy grin, introduced himself, and gave Holly an extravagant kiss, which practically made her swoon. Then he poured himself a large glass of wine and joined us. He was tall, in his mid-thirties, with wavy, dark-brown hair and piercing blue eyes. He had that offbeat artist look about him with his well-fitted jeans, worn leather boots, and tattoos peeking out of his casual button-down shirt.

Holly said proudly, "Daniel isn't just creating art, by the way, he's also very involved in the local art scene in Charleston. He advocates for artists."

Daniel gave a dismissive wave of his hand, but I could tell he was pleased at the praise. "I like giving back. The art community has been very supportive of me. It wouldn't be right for me not to be supportive back. It's sort of my way of paying it forward."

Grayson leaned in. "What kinds of things do you do?"

Daniel quirked a brow at him. "With the art community? Or with my art?"

"Both."

Daniel seemed to puff up at the interest. "I do a little bit of everything, in terms of art. If I'm not experimenting, I don't feel like I'm growing. I like exploring new techniques, styles, and concepts. If you don't keep pushing yourself, you stagnate in this business." He snorted and shared a look with Holly. "Like that landscape painter we talked to at that show."

Holly interjected again, that same note of pride in her voice. "There's nothing Daniel can't do. He's a multi-media artist. He sculpts just as well as he paints. And he's always coming up with fresh ideas and novel approaches. He's really an inspiration and a mentor to a lot of Charleston artists."

There was definitely a bit of hero-worship on Holly's end. I hoped Daniel felt the same way about her. Holly deserved nothing less.

"I like the idea of pushing boundaries," said Daniel.

"Are you mostly pursuing modern art?" I asked.

Daniel shrugged. "I just pursue whatever interests me at the time. Sometimes I'll put out some really traditional work, too. It depends on what I feel like." He glanced at his watch.

Holly continued talking up Daniel's artwork and how he was an inspiration to other local artists. Daniel kept interrupting her and correcting her. I felt myself tense.

There were a few moments of silence when none of us seemed to know what to say. Then Holly said brightly, "Grayson is a newspaper editor and Ann is a research librarian."

He gave us both smiles that didn't reach to his eyes. He didn't ask any questions, or seem very interested in our jobs. But then, I suppose they didn't sound like the most interesting of occupations, although they were to Grayson and me.

We were stuck again with a bit of silence since Daniel hadn't picked up the ball to ask us anything about our work. Grayson, always more outgoing than I was, quickly filled in. "Ann and I were excited to hear about your engagement. Have you made many plans? I always hear the toughest thing is finding a venue for the wedding or the reception, especially around the time you want the wedding to be. When are you planning on having the wedding?"

Holly flushed and looked over at Daniel as if waiting for him to answer that one.

Daniel said in a lazy voice, "We're taking it as it comes. Sometimes I feel like there's too much emphasis on planning. You can really suck the life out of an event like a wedding, you know? And weddings have gotten ridiculous—so much hoopla. In a lot of ways, I think it would be more fitting for Holly and me to start our life together by just going to the courthouse. We'd avoid all the needless planning, all the focus on unimportant details. 'Life is what happens when you're busy making other plans,' as John Lennon would say."

It was a quotation misattributed to Lennon and actually originated by writer and cartoonist Allen Saunders, a fact I decided to keep to myself. I also wasn't totally sure what Daniel was trying to say. Was he against large weddings? Or was he against planning?

Holly, perhaps sensing that Daniel was sounding like he was blowing off the wedding, quickly said, "We're thinking about a spring wedding. Charleston is beautiful in the spring."

Daniel shrugged again, as if the wedding wasn't his current focus. I guessed he was going to let Holly shoulder the planning. If it was going to be a spring wedding, and it was already September, there would have to be some planning soon.

Holly was looking increasingly uncomfortable, so I was glad when Grayson changed the subject. "How are things going at work, Holly? Are you still just as busy as ever?"

Holly gave him a relieved look and started talking about a change in management, increased responsibilities, and an excessive number of meetings, while Daniel did not try to hide the fact that he was on his phone and not listening to Holly at all.

I was surprised when Holly asked, "Is anybody ready for supper? I'm guessing you two just ate on the go this afternoon?"

It hadn't seemed that late in the day, but sure enough, it was after six. Daniel quickly said, "Sorry, I've got a dinner with the art council tonight. I'll take a raincheck on supper."

I saw a flicker of frustration or irritation in Holly's eyes. She clearly thought that Grayson's and my arrival should pre-empt other plans Daniel might have. I said, "Oh, that's no problem. And I could eat anytime."

Right then, though, just to tattle on me, my stomach gave a menacing growl. Everyone laughed, and I shrugged. "I really didn't think I was hungry until Holly mentioned supper. In fact, I can't believe it's after six. How about you, Grayson?"

"While you did a great job packing some really excellent snacks for the car, I could probably use something to eat, too."

Daniel stood, smiling. "I'll head out now and let you figure out your plans. Good meeting you both."

Chapter Three

After he left, Holly said, "Okay, here are our choices. I can make my famous spaghetti, or we can go out to someplace cool to eat. As you probably remember from last time, there's no shortage of great restaurants here."

I said, "We don't want to make you cook, Holly. We're here to celebrate your engagement. Having you working in the kitchen seems like it violates the spirit of the occasion."

Holly snorted. "It doesn't, believe me. Anyway, I kind of fancy spaghetti, and I like the way I make it."

Grayson said, "You hooked me with the words 'famous spaghetti.' I'm in."

I was secretly relieved. I'd had a busy morning at work, followed by a long car ride. I was going to be very social most of the time I was in Charleston. Having a quiet evening at home with Holly sounded like a plan.

We headed inside with a still-worn-out Murphy trotting happily ahead of us. I went upstairs to see if Fitz was ready to come out and socialize. He was, quickly padding downstairs to greet everyone. He watched Murphy with interest. The golden retriever practically tiptoed up to Fitz, delicately sticking his nose out to smell the cat. Fitz allowed this with remarkable good humor. But then, Fitz was the most laid-back of cats. With that, the two animals seemed to pick up where they left off, which was respectful disinterest.

Grayson and I offered to help with the food prep, and Holly took us up on it. While Holly browned the ground beef, she had Grayson chopping onions while I started a pot of water boiling. Murphy watched us from the corner with a big smile and a hopeful expression on his face. Holly whipped up her special homemade spaghetti sauce, which she said had been passed down by her grandmother. It seemed to feature fresh herbs, savory spices, and a rich tomato base.

Holly was chatting with us as we worked, more about what she'd been up to at work, how she and Murphy were attending dog training classes together, and her escapes to the beach when she could. As she talked, I realized she seemed very relaxed and happy. I wished I could see what Holly saw in Daniel. He was a good-looking guy, for sure, and sounded like he was very talented, to boot. I just hadn't gotten the warm-fuzzies when we were talking with him. But I also knew I had absolutely no business speaking my mind. For all I knew, Daniel had just had a long day and hadn't been at the top of his game.

After we had a great meal comprising delicious food and lively conversation, Grayson left Holly and me to catch up with each other and retired upstairs with his book and Fitz.

Holly gave me a somewhat anxious look. "So what did you think of Daniel?" The worried expression made me wonder if maybe she realized Daniel might not have made the best impression.

I smiled at her. "You both look very happy together. And when you're happy, I'm happy." It was as diplomatic of an answer as I could manage.

Holly relaxed a little. "We *are* really happy. We've been spending tons of time together lately, and I've felt like I was over-the-moon the whole time."

"How did the two of you meet?" This was something I was very curious about. Although Holly enjoyed art, she'd never been part of that scene before, at least as far as I was aware.

Holly's expression softened, remembering. "It was totally serendipitous. A friend of mine had a showing in one of the galleries. You know I don't know a lot about art, and I've never really been part of that scene. But I wanted to go and support my friend. It wasn't only her show—there were other artists there."

I said, "And one of the other artists was Daniel?"

Holly gave a reminiscent smile. "That's when I first laid eyes on him. He was one of the featured artists that night, and there was something about him that just immediately grabbed my attention. He was wearing this fitted black button-down shirt with dark jeans. I don't know—he just seemed so confident, like he knew he belonged there." Holly chuckled. "I felt totally different, of course. I wasn't at all at home there and felt really awkward. But he came over to talk to me. Asked me about art. I was so nervous that I just babbled on, saying I didn't know anything about art. He didn't make me feel bad about that at all. Instead, he asked me how the art made me *feel*."

"That sounds like a great way to not just talk about art, but to get something out of it," I said.

Holly gave an enthusiastic nod. "Exactly. Because no one can argue with what you *feel*, right? It's completely personal. And it's cool to think that different people can go into a gallery exhibit and get totally different, individual takeaways from the experience. Anyway, Daniel and I clicked right away. He made me feel like I was the most important person in the room. After the show, we just kept talking. We ended up at an all-night diner and sat there with plates of breakfast food and coffees and talked to each other for hours." She shrugged. "The rest is history."

"I'm so excited for you," I said. "You've got to be looking forward to starting your new life together." This was as close as I wanted to come to asking about the currently murky date for the wedding.

"I definitely am. Daniel has a few things he's got to wrap up, work-wise, before we start planning the wedding. He said he didn't want work hanging over him while we were pulling all the details together."

I nodded. Murphy came over and put his head on Holly's lap as if he realized she needed reassurance. Holly stroked his head, and the dog looked up at her soulfully.

Holly latched onto a different subject. I felt bad for her because I guessed that whenever Holly saw her friends or talked with people at work, the big question on everybody's lips was going to be when they needed to save the date for the wedding. She said, "Enough about me. What are you and Grayson planning on doing while you're here? Anything you especially want to do or see in Charleston? Beside me, of course," she added with a laugh.

I gave her a rueful look. "Well, my boss gave me an assignment that I need to tackle while I'm here." I pulled out my phone. "I should probably check my emails and see if the woman I'm meeting has set up a time for me to talk to her."

"Library business in Charleston?"

I said, "I know. It sounds unlikely, but Wilson somehow made it happen." I scanned my emails and opened one from Bianca Donovan. "Looks like she's inviting me over to coffee at her place tomorrow morning. I guess she doesn't mind having me interrupt her Saturday morning."

Holly said, "Great! Nice and early so you can have the rest of the day to do whatever you want."

"Exactly. Thank goodness. The last thing I wanted to do on my vacation is work. And to answer your question, Grayson and I are really open. We want to hang out with you, of course, and get to know Daniel better. Aside from that, Grayson is planning on running by his uncle's old house to see if he can go through some of his things. Other than that, we don't have any plans at all."

The last time we'd come to Charleston together, Grayson's uncle had just passed away. To Grayson's surprise, he'd left him a considerable estate, including his house. Now Grayson would need to clear the property to sell it. It was a big job and not something he seemed in a hurry to tackle.

"Sounds like time for both fun and being productive," said Holly.

I quickly emailed Bianca back, then, business concluded, I put my phone away to catch up with my friend.

The next morning, the sun streamed through the window. I opened a sleepy eye to see what time it was. It was already seven-thirty, and I groaned. I had planned on getting up earlier and taking a walk with Holly before meeting up with Bianca Donovan for our meeting. I must have been more tired out from the trip than I thought. Plus, Holly and I had stayed up late, talking.

Grayson was already up and downstairs. I could hear him chatting with Holly. He must have fed Fitz, too, because he had a little food still left in his bowl and was contentedly curled next to me. I rubbed him for a few minutes, hearing him purr happily and roll over onto his back. He was one of the few cats it was safe to give a tummy rub to. Then I slipped out of the bed and into the shower. I pulled on a business professional mix of black slacks and a silky white blouse, dabbed on some makeup, and headed downstairs. I needed to eat something before meeting Bianca Donovan. Otherwise, my stomach might make some of the same rude noises it had yesterday.

"Good morning," chorused Grayson and Holly.

"Grayson made us pancakes," said Holly.

"Out of Holly's provisions," said Grayson with a grin. "That means it qualifies as a team effort. Have a seat."

I did, and he brought a stack of pancakes, which he placed in front of me with a flourish. I poured some maple syrup over them and dug into them hungrily.

Holly said, "Good luck with your work thing. What is it exactly?"

I washed down a big bite of pancakes with the coffee Grayson had put in front of me. "It's supposed to be an information-gathering conversation. I can't remember how much I told you last night. She's the state archaeologist and she's supposed to give me ideas on how to word a citizen survey for better engagement."

Holly frowned. "State archeologist. Wait a minute. Is she Bianca Donovan?"

"The very one. You mean you know her?"

Holly shook her head quickly. "Not really. I mainly just know who she is. I've heard her speaking on the local news before, and she sounds really sharp. You'll probably have a more interesting meeting than you're thinking you will."

"Good to know. I'm thinking it shouldn't last too long, at any rate. Wilson has become interested in collaborating with our town on historic preservation. It's definitely a worthwhile project and something I'm interested in. I just wasn't excited about having it dumped on me at the last minute."

We chatted for a few more minutes before I hurried out the door, setting my GPS to Bianca's address and hopping into Grayson's car. It looked like, with morning traffic, it was going to take me twenty minutes to get there.

Twenty minutes later, I pulled into Bianca's driveway. It looked like she had a historic house herself, which was aligned with her interest in history. It was a tall and narrow two-story Georgian home with red brick and white trim. She had a beautifully well-tended garden with Encore azalea bushes blooming.

I walked up the path to the front door and rang the doorbell. After a minute, with no answer, I knocked on the door. I waited another minute without an answer. Maybe Bianca was in the restroom. I rang the doorbell again with no response.

Then I walked around to the other side of the house, just in case Bianca was out of earshot in the backyard or on a patio. She might have lost track of the time or even nodded off, considering it was still early on a Saturday morning. But there was no one there.

I knocked loudly, one more time at the front door. This time, the front door slid open under the force of my fist. It hadn't been all the way closed. I cautiously poked my head inside. "Dr. Donovan? It's Ann Beckett. From the library?"

There was no answer. But now, the little hairs on the back of my neck were standing up. Something just didn't feel right. It was too quiet. I called out again, louder, but got no response.

I walked farther into the house, moving toward what looked like a living room. And there, lying on the floor, was the body of a woman.

Chapter Four

I hurried over to check for a pulse. I couldn't feel one, but noticed the woman's skin was still warm. Her dark hair was pulled back into a ponytail, and she was wearing a V-neck tee shirt and a pair of cotton shorts. She was lying in front of a chair, as if she'd fallen out of it. I saw some redness around her neck, which made me wonder.

I stepped back, carefully made my way out of the house, and with shaking hands, pulled out my phone to call the police.

I waited, sitting in my front seat, for the cops to arrive. I didn't completely trust my legs to hold me up. Was that Bianca Donovan? I googled her name on my phone and pulled up an image that matched the woman I'd seen on the floor. Yes, that had been Bianca. Could it possibly have been a natural death? There hadn't been any blood or signs of a fight. The house had been tidy, and it didn't look as if anything, at least in the living room, had been rifled through, so it seemed unlikely to be a break-in. At the same time, she'd seemed young and fit and not someone likely to be the victim of a heart attack or other natural death.

The police pulled up, along with both an ambulance and a fire truck, for good measure. They had me move my car out to the street, something I should have thought of myself. The police, naturally, asked me to wait to speak with them. A minute later, they were already stringing up crime scene tape.

I was so engrossed by watching the emergency workers that a tap on my window made me jump. A woman around sixty-years-old was standing there with concern in her hazel eyes. Figuring she was a neighbor, I turned on the car and rolled down the window.

"I'm Eleanor Johnson," the woman said in a cultured voice. "Is something wrong with Bianca?" She leaned forward, frowning at me, and her salt-and-pepper bob framed her face.

I took a deep breath. "Is she a friend of yours?"

I detected the slightest bit of hesitation before Eleanor said, "I've known Bianca for a while. What's happened?" Now her voice was impatient. She looked like someone accustomed to getting what she wanted. Although she was dressed simply in a crisp white blouse and tailored trousers, I could tell both items probably cost more than even the fanciest clothes I owned.

I cleared my throat. "I'm sorry. I'm afraid Bianca is dead."

"*Dead*? But how? She was a young woman," said Eleanor, looking with those piercing eyes at Bianca's house as if she could see through the walls and find out what was going on by herself.

"I don't really know," I said.

Eleanor now looked at me skeptically. "Did you find her?"

"I did."

Eleanor tilted her head to one side. "What were you doing here? Are you a friend of Bianca's?"

I shook my head. "I was supposed to meet with her for something related to my work. Bianca didn't answer her door, and I walked in to call for her."

Eleanor pursed her lips. "I see."

She turned to see a tall, blond man in suit pants and a button-down shirt striding toward us. "I should go," she murmured.

But the man, a detective, politely asked Eleanor to stay. He introduced himself as Ethan Morrow of the Charleston police. I stepped out of the car and Morrow led us to a shady spot for our conversation. A little shade was welcome since, despite the fact it was September, the air had heated up and the humidity had kicked in accordingly.

"I really have to be going," said Eleanor apologetically to Morrow. "Perhaps I can speak with you later?"

Morrow smiled at her. "It won't take long. Just a few questions now, then I'll contact you later if I need a follow-up." He took our contact information, raising his eyebrow a little when I gave him an out-of-state address.

Then he turned to Eleanor. "Ms. Johnson. What was your purpose for being here this morning?"

Eleanor retained her poise, although I saw her finger her necklace a bit nervously. The necklace, which rested on her white blouse, was a stunning pendant with what looked like an intricately designed family crest set in gleaming silver. "I was planning to meet with Bianca. When I drove up, I saw all the commotion outside her house. Then I saw this young woman and stopped to see if she knew what happened. I understand Bianca's the one who's deceased?"

Morrow glanced at me for a second. "You identified the body?"

I gave a slight shake of my head. "Only by looking up Bianca Donovan online to view a photo of her. She and I were to have a meeting this morning, but I'd never met her."

Morrow quirked his brow again, now turning to Eleanor. "It seems odd that Ms. Donovan would schedule two meetings at the same time. And on a weekend, at that."

Eleanor looked impatient again, as if she was someone who wasn't used to being questioned. "Bianca wasn't expecting me. I was just in the neighborhood and decided to drop in for a quick chat. As I mentioned, I then saw all the emergency vehicles and this young woman. I wanted to find out what was going on."

"How do you know Ms. Donovan?" asked Morrow.

Eleanor took a deep breath, looking off to the side. "We're acquainted with each other via our shared historic interests," she drawled. "Bianca was the state archaeologist."

"And you're a historian?"

Eleanor quickly said, "An amateur one." Then, as if realizing she might need to correct the record even more, she said, "My interest is rather limited in scope. I'm focused on my family's history." She fingered the pendant with the family crest again.

The detective tilted his head as if his memory was being jogged. Understanding dawned in Morrow's eyes. "That's right. It's been covered in the local news quite a bit recently. Can't really get away from it, actually. Let's see if I can remember the details." He looked thoughtful for a moment. But somehow, I got the impression that he recalled quite a bit about Eleanor's involvement with Bianca Donovan.

Eleanor cut in. "It's really nothing. She and I are barely acquainted."

Morrow's gaze remained fixed on Eleanor, his expression inscrutable as he processed her responses. "But you're acquainted enough for you to drop in on her unannounced fairly early in the day?"

Eleanor looked displeased. "Bianca knew I was coming by at some point. She simply didn't know when."

"What was your visit concerning?"

"I can't see where that's any of your business," said Eleanor huffily.

"Unfortunately, with a suspicious death, everything becomes my business."

Eleanor's eyes opened wide. "So her death is suspicious?"

"We have to identify it as such, temporarily. The medical examiner will tell us more." Morrow looked expectantly at Eleanor.

Eleanor was quiet for a moment. "Bianca found something related to my family's history. Something in the library archive when she was researching. She was planning on sharing it with me. That's all it was."

Morrow said, "Did Ms. Donovan tell you what she'd discovered?"

"Actually," said Eleanor crisply, "it's *Dr.* Donovan. And no, she didn't tell me. Which explains why I was here."

Eleanor's face was flushed, and she didn't look at Morrow as she spoke. I couldn't help but get the impression she wasn't telling the truth about why she'd been at Bianca's house.

Morrow continued, "From what I remember, your family lay claim to land in Charleston. In a highly desirable area, I believe."

"Heritage Grove," said Eleanor with a sniff.

"Yes. But an archaeologist said it was public property with historic significance. I'm guessing that must have been Dr. Donovan."

Eleanor's face flushed with anger. "The land is privately-owned property. Family property. We've always had ancestral ties to Heritage Grove. We were the original settlers of the area. We didn't *lay claim* to the land, as you put it. We own it."

Morrow wagged a pen he was holding at Eleanor. "Except Dr. Donovan's research found otherwise, didn't it? She discovered artifacts on the property, which she sought historical designation for. And she wanted it to be open to the public."

"She didn't know what she was talking about," snapped Eleanor, her voice dripping with disdain. "My family has stories about Heritage Grove dating back generations. Any artifacts are the family's."

Morrow watched Eleanor's agitation curiously, his expression betraying a hint of amusement at her indignation. He said thoughtfully, "I believe there might even recently have been a lawsuit initiated."

"Only to protect what's ours." Eleanor's eyes flashed defiantly.

Morrow nodded calmly, unfazed by Eleanor's defensiveness. "Got it. Bianca Donovan and your family were at odds because of a land dispute."

"It's not a dispute," said Eleanor stiffly. Her eyes narrowed. "You're not presuming I have anything to do with whatever happened to Bianca? I barely even know the woman."

Morrow gave her an accessing look. "It's interesting that you knew where she lived."

Eleanor threw a well-manicured hand in the air. "I know where many people live! It doesn't mean I murder them."

"I'm just following general procedure," said Morrow in a soothing voice. "Where were you earlier this morning?"

"Me? Well, I was at home, naturally. Going through some family artifacts and organizing them. And drinking my coffee, eating a bowl of cereal, and getting ready for my day."

Morrow asked, "Can anyone vouch for that?"

Eleanor looked most unhappy that she was being asked for an alibi. "Unfortunately not. My husband Charles was giving a presentation at the rotary club breakfast this morning. My son Will is on a fishing trip."

Morrow nodded. "A fishing trip off the Charleston coast?"

"No, in North Carolina. He's with a group of anglers that's booked a fishing charter near Wrightsville Beach."

Morrow jotted down a couple of notes in a small notebook. He said in a casual voice, "What did you make of Bianca Donovan?"

"What did I *make* of her? I didn't think of her one way or another. That wasn't any of my business." Her tone was dismissive, a clear indication that she wanted to move past the subject quickly.

Morrow said in the same calm tone, "You must have made some sort of impression of her. It would help me a lot to get some sort of handle on her as a person."

Eleanor blew out a sigh. But it was clear she was more willing to talk about Bianca after Morrow framed it as "being helpful." She said, "Well, she could occasionally be a difficult person to get along with." Eleanor was clearly carefully picking her words, but it was obvious from her tight expression that she'd disliked Bianca. "But she was incredibly professional at her work. She was an excellent speaker—you can find some of her lectures online if you look her up. Naturally, being an excellent researcher came with the territory. I believe she must have been quite meticulous with her research. She cared passionately about what she was doing and fought to do what she thought was right."

Morrow nodded, encouragingly. "Is there an instance in particular where Dr. Donovan fought for something she believed in?"

Eleanor gave him an exasperated look. "Well, the Stone Fleet, of course. Naturally. The sand replenishment. All of that. Absolutely no one wanted to preserve the Stone Fleet, aside from Bianca. It's rotting away in the ocean, for heaven's sake."

I had no idea what the Stone Fleet was, but Morrow nodded again.

Eleanor went on. "There's going to be a community meeting on the Stone Fleet tomorrow at the library. Of course, Bianca was supposed to be the key speaker there to protect it. I wonder who'll step in now. I've no doubt that guy Nolan will be there."

"Nolan?" asked Morrow.

"Oh, he's an amateur archaeologist, although you'd think he'd gotten a PhD in the subject if you listen to him. He clearly thinks a lot of himself. He and Bianca couldn't stand each other. There was some sort of controversy over something Nolan found and the way he found it. Bianca disapproved." Eleanor shrugged to show that was all she knew about that.

Morrow jotted down another note. "Do you have any ideas who else might have had problems with Bianca Donovan?"

Eleanor now looked directly at me and gave a sniff. "Well, I'd like to know who this woman is and why she was in Bianca's house."

Morrow turned to me, as well. He'd already collected my personal information, so I didn't repeat my name. "I'm a librarian from Whitby, North Carolina. My library director asked me to arrange a meeting with Dr. Donovan in order to get information on her methods to increase engagement with community surveys."

Eleanor's eyes glazed over just the slightest bit. Morrow didn't seem particularly interested either, although he jotted down more notes.

"So you'd never met her," said Morrow.

"That's right. She'd invited me to come over to her house this morning to talk and have coffee. When she didn't answer her door at nine-thirty, I continued knocking and ringing the doorbell. It was important to my director that I have this meeting, and it seemed odd that Dr. Donovan wasn't answering the door. Then I walked inside and found her." I swallowed, my throat suddenly dry.

Morrow asked for Wilson's name and contact information, presumably to check out the story. Then he turned to Eleanor again. "You were going to give me names of people who might have had an issue with Bianca."

"I've already given you the name of that Nolan guy. Bianca thought he was an idiot, but he was on Bianca's side when it came to preserving historic sites. For the most part." Now Eleanor looked impatient. "And that's really all I know. I'd like to leave now. It's been a most trying morning."

Chapter Five

E leanor left but Morrow indicated he wanted to ask me a few more questions. "May I ask what you're in town for? I see your permanent address is in North Carolina. Were you only in town for this meeting with Dr. Donovan?"

"My college roommate is getting married, and I'm here with my boyfriend for a visit and to meet her fiancé," I said. I was now starting to feel like this trip was becoming a lot more complicated than it had started out.

"Is there anyone who can vouch for your whereabouts this morning?"

Thankfully, this part was straightforward. "Yes. My boyfriend and my former roommate. We're staying with her while we're in town." Then I gave him their contact information.

"I'm a little surprised you entered the house, considering you didn't know Dr. Donovan and you were here for a work trip. Were you concerned about her?" Morrow asked.

I thought about this for a moment. "I don't know if I was concerned about her, really. I didn't have any reason to believe anything had happened to Dr. Donovan. But I was definitely concerned about getting the appointment with her out of the way. I'm here for vacation and to see my friend, and I wanted to take care of the task my boss had given me. Also, I was confused about why Dr. Donovan had set up a meeting and then not answered her door when it was time."

"You thought it was out of character?"

"Well, I've never met her, of course, so I wouldn't know that. But it didn't seem organized or professional. Plus, she was a relative of my director's friend. It just seemed unlikely that she'd have forgotten the meeting. She'd only just set it up yesterday, after all."

Morrow said, "So you walked inside."

"Yes. It wasn't exactly as awful as it sounds. After a lot of doorbell ringing, a walk around the side of the house, and some fairly gentle tapping at the front door, I pounded on the door. It opened."

Morrow made a note of this. "It sounds like it wasn't really even shut well, then?"

"I guess not."

Morrow said, "How much did you disturb the body?"

"Only enough to check for a pulse and make sure an ambulance wasn't needed." I paused. "There wasn't any blood or signs of violence that I could see, so I thought maybe Dr. Donovan had passed out. I called the police as soon as I realized she was dead."

Morrow made another note in his notebook. "Got it. Okay, I know you're eager to get on with your vacation, so I'll let you go. But I'll be in touch if I have any further questions. And, of course, I'll be speaking with your friend, boyfriend, and director."

I nodded and headed to my car, happy to be away from his piercing eyes. I had the feeling I was going to be eliminated from the suspect pool quickly, but it was still pretty unnerving. And the mention of Wilson made me realize I'd need to call him and update him on what happened. I started dialing before I'd pulled off the street.

"Ann?" asked Wilson. It sounded like he was frowning. "Aren't you meeting with Bianca Donovan now? Or is the meeting already over?"

"I'm afraid the meeting didn't happen at all." I quickly explained. There was silence on the other end as Wilson digested the news. "I'm sorry. I know you're friends of her family."

"Her uncle," said Wilson absently. He cleared his throat. "What horrible news. And it seems like foul play, you say?

"The police are treating it that way until they find out differently."

Wilson said, "I'm guessing the police will want to notify the family, then. I shouldn't call my friend."

"I wouldn't, no. They'll want to speak with Dr. Donovan's parents first, of course, to let them know. It wouldn't be good if they found out from a non-official source."

Wilson sighed. "A terrible tragedy. And an awful scene for you to come across. On your vacation, as well. I'm sorry, Ann."

I said, "Maybe we can think of a different approach for the historic preservation project. Consulting with local historians, maybe. Even amateur historians."

"Yes. I'll consider that. I do think the survey is a good idea still, even though I'm not sure the best way to get more engagement with it. But I believe we should put it on the back burner for a little while. Mull it over. And Ann? Try to put this all out of your head. Enjoy your time away."

I thanked him and hung up. The traffic was busier on the way back, and I was glad to be off the phone and concentrating on my driving and the GPS directions.

When I got back to Holly's house, she was just coming back from a walk with Murphy. It was already humid outside, despite it being September, and beads of sweat dotted her face. Murphy was panting, then his mouth stretched into a doggy grin when he saw me getting out of Grayson's car.

"Hey there boy," I crooned to him. It felt good to give him a cuddle, and I put my arms around him and laying my head in his soft fur.

"How did your meeting go?" asked Holly, as we walked down her driveway.

"Well, it didn't go as expected," I said. "In fact, everything is kind of a mess."

I filled her in quickly, as I had Wilson. But Holly sounded a lot more distressed. I found out why in a minute.

"You're saying Bianca Donovan is dead?"

"I'm sorry, Holly. I didn't get the impression you really knew her."

Holly sank onto the sofa. "Yeah. At least, I know *of* her. She used to date Daniel."

My first reaction was . . . no way. But Charleston was such a closed, sort of cliquey community. "Wow. Okay. Was that recently that they were involved?"

"Not in the far distant past, no. Obviously not *very* recently." Holly stared at me. "I can't believe you're back in Charleston and caught up in another murder investigation."

"I know. I'm hoping I'll be cleared pretty quickly. It didn't help that I found the body."

Holly put her hand over her mouth. "Oh my gosh, of course you did. I'm sorry—are you okay? Do you want a drink? Water? Something stronger? I could make us bloody Marys."

"No, I'm okay, thanks. I was mainly mentioning it because the cops will be calling you and Grayson soon to check my whereabouts this morning. Just a heads-up."

Holly said wryly, "Well, that's easy. You were a sleepyhead and didn't wake up until it was practically time for your meeting. I think your alibi is covered." She ran a hand through her hair. "This is so crazy, though. Daniel's not going to believe it when I tell him." Her face was grim as she thought about filling Daniel in.

We were quiet for a few moments, then I said, "There was a woman who came up to the scene when she saw all the emergency vehicles. Someone who knew Bianca. Eleanor Johnson."

Holly rolled her eyes. "It feels like she's everywhere right now. She's been on the local news and in the paper all the time. It's like that old house and property is her life's work."

"Maybe it is," I said. "She sounded really passionate about it."

"The thing is," said Holly, wagging her finger, "it's not even *her* family. I mean, it is, but only by marriage. But boy, her face is all over the news. She's taking the family's land very, very seriously."

"There was something she and the police officer were talking about that I didn't understand. They made a reference to some kind of rock or something."

Holly frowned. "A rock?"

"Or maybe a stone. Something to do with historical preservation? And Bianca Donovan."

"Ohhh," said Holly, nodding. "Now I know what you're talking about. The Stone Fleet."

"That was it. What's all that about?"

"Another big controversy, of course. Charleston is rife with them. You could probably find out more about it at the library than by getting information from me. I've just casually kept up with it. Basically, Isle of Palms needed to replenish its beach, which had washed away. I think a lot of the sand there had actually washed over to Sullivan's Island. Anyway, they were going to dredge the sand out of the ocean and build up the beach with it."

I said slowly, "And they discovered something out in the ocean?"

"Bingo. It was a Union blockade. There were some old whaling vessels that the Union loaded with rock as part of its blockade during the Civil War. Bianca was very involved with the discovery and the research following it."

I said, "Okay. So that stopped the sand replenishment for that section. But why couldn't they find another spot off the coast to use? It's not like there isn't plenty of ocean."

"From what I remember, there weren't a lot of other choices. Apparently, there isn't much sand off the island that's an appropriate grade to be poured on the beach."

I said, "Eleanor Johnson mentioned something about there being a public hearing on the Stone Fleet."

Holly dug out her phone and said, "Looks like it's tomorrow, midday. If you're interested in it, maybe you should go. It's actually going to be at the library—you could find out more about the Stone Fleet in the historical archives, then hear the bickering about the beach replenishment at the meeting."

"That might be a good plan. If Bianca stood in the way of the sand replenishment, she might really have gotten on somebody's bad side."

"Oh, totally. And I'm just skimming the surface in terms of all the back-and-forth on this stuff. There's so much money involved with beach replenishment. You have wealthy homeowners, developers . . . just all kinds of interests. It sounds like Bianca was playing with fire." Holly paused, looking distracted. "Anyway, it would be a lot better, obviously, if Bianca was targeted because of her work as an archaeologist than if she was targeted personally."

"You said you don't know much about Bianca's relationship with Daniel, right?"

Holly was quiet for a moment. "That's right. But Daniel and I have run into Bianca when we've been out around town. I've always felt a little intimidated by her. Clearly, she's super-smart and ambitious. But she always seemed like she had a really ethical core. Maybe a personal code of ethics. If the cops start digging into Bianca's personal life, which I'm sure they will, then Daniel is definitely going to be a suspect."

"Maybe not," I said lightly. "After all, Daniel has obviously moved on. The two of you are getting married."

Holly looked away, seeming uncomfortable. I wondered again if the engagement was going to be a long one. "Yeah. But Ann, public opinion is something else. Everybody knows Daniel and Bianca used to date. They were a pretty high-profile couple in town. There is going to be whispering, gossip. How can we get married under a haze of suspicion? The police need to solve the case first. Put somebody behind bars."

I frowned a little. Putting off a wedding until Bianca's murderer was caught sounded pretty extreme for Holly. After all, Daniel and Bianca weren't even currently involved. "Okay."

Holly gave me a crooked smile. "I know how that sounds. The problem is my family. They're not totally onboard with Daniel."

I loved Holly's mom and dad, but I could see where they might not be delighted about Daniel. They were very traditional, monied people. Plus, they'd recently lost Holly's brother. It didn't surprise me that they might be over-protective of Holly. And they definitely wanted the best for her. I wondered if Daniel just had a way of making a bad first impression.

Holly continued. "My folks look at Daniel as somebody who pushes the boundaries."

"With his art?"

"With everything," said Holly drolly. "He's covered in tattoos, for one. And he often doesn't have much of a filter during conversations. They've never said anything to me, but I can see the disapproval in their eyes and manner. They're pretty easy to read."

"I'm sure they like the way he makes you happy," I said. Holly had seemed like she was on cloud nine yesterday when she was around Daniel. It was the one thing that made me feel good about their relationship.

"I'm sure they do," said Holly quickly, although she didn't sound totally convinced.

Chapter Six

Holly's front door swung open, and Daniel came striding in. He seemed to be in a very upbeat mood. He gave Holly a quick kiss, gave me a charming crooked grin, then headed for the coffeepot. "How are things?" he asked as he poured himself a mug of coffee along with a generous helping of sugar.

Holly and I exchanged glances. Holly said, "Actually, I've got some bad news."

Daniel turned, frowning. "What happened?"

"It's Bianca. She's ... passed away."

Daniel's frown deepened. "Passed *away*? What? Was she in a car accident or something? I haven't heard anything about her being sick or anything."

Holly looked over at me. I cleared my throat. "Unfortunately, it might be a case of foul play. At least, the police are treating it like a suspicious death for now."

Daniel sat abruptly on one of the kitchen chairs. "I don't understand. When did this happen?" He directed the question my way.

"This morning. I had a meeting set up with Bianca for work—my work at the library. When she didn't answer the door, I walked into her house and found her. I'm sorry. Holly was telling me that you were friends of hers."

Daniel gave a short laugh. "*Friends* is far too simple of a word to describe what Bianca and I were." He looked down at the coffee mug. "I might need something else to drink. Does anyone want a bloody Mary? I made a batch yesterday that's still in the fridge."

Holly and I shook our heads, so Daniel made himself one, still throwing questions at me. He'd seemed totally incurious about my work the day before, but was now peppering me with questions about how my library job in North Carolina had intersected with Bianca's work here. After a few sips of his drink, he seemed more settled. It wasn't that he appeared upset at the news of Bianca's death, more like he was having a tough time absorbing the news.

He looked at Holly. "Well, the police are going to be in touch. Sooner rather than later."

"Maybe not," said Holly, although her expression belied her words.

Daniel shook his head. "They will. I promise you. Bianca and I had too many publicized tiffs and bad feelings between us. And everything spilled into social media, naturally, as these things do." He looked at me with a weary look on his face. "Bianca and I were engaged, too."

Holly hadn't shared that tidbit with me. Maybe she hadn't because she wanted it to look like Daniel wasn't a serial fiancé. I hoped they could set a wedding date soon, if Holly was feeling insecure at all on that score.

"When did this happen?" asked Daniel. "I mean, it sounds like this morning, but was it last night? Then Bianca was just found this morning?"

I shook my head. "That wasn't something the police shared with me." But I knew Bianca was still warm when I'd felt for a pulse. I decided to keep that information to myself.

"No, I guess they wouldn't." Daniel nibbled on a fingernail, thinking. He glanced over at Holly. "Anyway, if it was early this morning, you and I were together."

Holly looked startled. "This morning? Yeah, some of the time." She glanced over at me. "Daniel walked Murphy with me after I got up."

He said coolly, "Then I had to drive over to look at the progress being made on a mural restoration project downtown."

Holly's brow wrinkled. "Did anyone see you?"

Daniel hesitated. "Not that I noticed, but somebody might have."

I said, "You were both up early this morning. I really slept in for once." I'd said it in an easy tone, hoping to lighten the mood, but neither of them was listening. I'd have to ask Grayson later if Holly had been downstairs when he got up and made those pancakes.

"When was the last time you saw Bianca?" asked Holly.

Daniel blew out a breath. "Who knows? I've had minimal interaction with her for a long time. I've done my best to avoid her. She's just somebody I had a past history with. She was doing her thing with history, whatever that was. History is dead and buried, you know? I was doing my thing with art, something that's still alive, something impactful. We rarely crossed paths. Really, she's irrelevant."

I noticed the slightest bit of perspiration dotting his brow.

Holly said, "You and Bianca seem like you were so different. It's hard to imagine how the two of you were ever an item."

Daniel shrugged. "Yeah, true. We had different goals and different ideas for what was important for Charleston. I was all about expanding culture in the area. I wanted to get art into the schools, influence the next generation. I wanted to push Spoleto to be even bigger, better, pull more people in."

Spoleto was the huge Charleston arts festival that had been around for decades.

Daniel continued, "I wanted Charleston to be known as a cultural hub for the whole eastern seaboard, not just the South."

"And Bianca?" I asked.

"She was rigid when it came to historical preservation. Rigid when it came to arguing over funds and fund allocation." Daniel gave a short laugh. "I wanted to earmark a building for the arts, then Bianca discovered it was historic. But *everything* in Charleston is historic. It's a freaking old city. 1670? That's practically the Stone Age for America."

I said slowly, "So it sounds like the art community and the historic community could be at odds."

"All the time," said Daniel. "And plenty of people felt that way, not just me. I guess I was mostly the spokesperson on behalf of the arts, which is the problem. I'm the face of the art community here."

I must have looked a little lost, and Holly too, because Daniel sighed and launched into an explanation. "So, you can't do anything in Charleston without tripping over some kind of historic artifact. If you're renovating an old house? The contractors are going to find something. Got a new apartment building being built that you're preparing the ground for? Something's going to be found."

I said, "Holly was telling me about the Stone Fleet right before you came in."

"Exactly. Perfect example. Going to dredge up some sand from the ocean? Good luck! There's some historic old wood out there. Not that anyone can *see* the wood. Not that you can make a museum in the ocean so that people can visit it and think about the Union blockade. Nope. But it's got to be preserved. That's the thing—whenever there's an archaeological finding, it means more regulation. More bureaucracy. More hurdles for artists and everyone else to jump. We've got a rapidly evolving arts scene in town, and Bianca's pet projects meant excavations and restrictions on plots of land that would have worked for art spaces, galleries, or art installation."

There were more dots of perspiration joining the others. Daniel muttered, "The cops are going to be hounding me, all right." He looked over meaningfully at Holly, who looked away. I had the feeling Daniel was going to try to make sure Holly gave him a solid alibi.

I said, "It sounds like Bianca had the ability to get on people's bad sides. Can you think of someone else who'd had issues with her? Giving the police a better suspect would help divert attention away from you."

Daniel brightened at the thought. "True. Well, there's Sierra Barnett, of course."

"Who's she?"

Holly frowned. "She's the turtle team person, right?"

"The turtle team?" I asked. "Are those the people who help protect the sea turtles who come ashore to lay eggs?"

"That's right," said Holly.

Daniel said, "Sierra is really vocal, too, like me. The beach at Isle of Palms was getting smaller, which was an issue for the turtles. It meant that people and turtle eggs were sharing a narrow sliver of space. So she's in favor of the beach replenishment, along with all the other members of the turtle team."

I nodded. "Which pitted her against Bianca, I guess. Since Bianca was against the beach replenishment because of the Stone Fleet discovery."

Daniel said, "I don't think Bianca cared one way or another about the beach replenishment. The problem was that she didn't want the sand to come from *that* spot. If they wanted to dredge sand from somewhere else in the ocean, that was fine with her. But apparently, that was the best spot for the dredging to take place." He thought for a minute. "I bet Cooper is already getting bothered by the police, too."

Holly looked over at me. "Cooper Thornton is a local developer. A friend of Daniel's, actually."

Daniel bobbed his head. "He's a supporter of the arts, so I know him that way. Not only does he give money to local arts initiatives, he also *buys* a lot of art. He's got some of my stuff, too."

I said, "Was one of his developments threatened because of a historic find?"

Holly said, "Yep. The Stone Fleet was the find. He was wanting to develop a hotel right on the beach. He needed that sand replenishment project."

Daniel was looking down in the mouth again. "Still, are the cops going to pick on a local bigwig like Cooper Thornton? Or somebody like me? I'm thinking somebody like me."

Holly reached out for his hand. "*I* think you're a local bigwig."

"Yeah, but just in the arts community. The cops won't have a clue about that. This is bad, Holly."

Holly glanced over at me. "Remember how I was telling you that Ann had a knack for solving mysteries? Digging up dirt and figuring out who the perpetrators are?"

Daniel nodded, looking distracted.

"Well, she's going to do some poking around for us. Maybe she can find out more about who else might have had issues with Bianca. She'll tell the police, which will point them in a different direction. Relieve some of the pressure off of you."

Daniel muttered, "Maybe the pressure would be off of me if you gave me a better alibi." He gave Holly a dark look, got up, and walked out of the house.

Holly gave me a small smile after he stormed out. "I guess the artistic personality can be high-strung."

I thought it was just Daniel being a jerk. None of this was Holly's fault. And I didn't like the fact that he was trying to make Holly provide him with an alibi he clearly didn't have. But Holly was looking so stressed that I didn't say anything about it. Instead, I said, "How about if I head over to the library and get started with that poking around? The library is open on Sundays here, right?"

"I think so. But you think the library is the place to start?"

I said wryly, "I'm a research librarian. I *always* think the library is the place to start. I want to find out more about the Stone Fleet, in particular. I'm thinking a little background might help me out."

Grayson joined us a few minutes later and was interested in going to the library, too. I think both of us just wanted to give Holly some space. Grayson didn't realize just how much space Holly needed, because I decided not to tell him about what had happened until we got into the car.

We set out for the downtown library. Grayson said, "Hey, how did your meeting go?"

I grimaced. "I didn't want to go through it again with Holly there. But when I arrived at Bianca's house, things didn't go exactly as planned. I discovered her, dead."

"*What?*"

I launched through the story again. I didn't mind reciting it because telling what happened helped to normalize it more for me and make it less frightening. But Grayson could still tell how bad it must have been.

"I can't believe it," he said slowly. "I'm so sorry."

"Thanks. I know I didn't meet her, but she's kind of coming to life with all the stories I've been hearing about her from different people."

Grayson said, "What have you been hearing?"

"I think she must have been a real professional. She cared a lot about historical preservation and was willing to fight for what she believed in. The only problem with that is that it put her on people's bad sides. Bianca was the person who was holding up development, beach renourishment projects . . . things like that."

I took a deep breath. "And there's another thing. Bianca dated Daniel. Actually, she was engaged to him."

Grayson took his eyes off the road briefly. "You're kidding."

"I'm afraid not. Apparently, they've had a contentious relationship since the breakup, too. Bianca stepped in and nixed a space Daniel was trying to acquire for artists. He's worried the police are going to consider him a suspect because of all the times he and Bianca were on opposite sides."

Grayson gave a low whistle. "Poor Holly."

"Poor Holly for a lot of reasons." I paused. "What do you make of Daniel?"

Grayson sighed. "Well, I've only met him the one time. I can't really say."

"But your first impression?"

Grayson said, "It wasn't great. He seemed sort of self-centered."

"Right. I thought the same thing. I was willing to give him a pass yesterday because sometimes first impressions are misleading. We got a really limited glimpse at Daniel. He might have had a rough day or his mind might have been elsewhere. Or maybe he's shy and doesn't handle meeting people well."

"Or maybe he's self-centered," said Grayson with an impish grin.

"Yeah, true."

"You said you were willing to give him a pass yesterday. Did something else happen today when you saw him?" asked Grayson.

"What really bothered me this morning is that he was pressuring Holly to give him an alibi."

Grayson shook his head. "Not good."

"Nope. I could tell Holly felt conflicted over it."

"Did he have no alibi at all? Or just a bad one?" asked Grayson.

"Daniel said that he was out checking on an art installation. But nobody can confirm that, apparently." I hesitated and said, "Aside from the stuff related to the murder, it bothers me that there's no date for the wedding. Especially since Daniel was engaged before and didn't get married."

Grayson said, "The wedding date is probably one of those things that comes later, though, doesn't it? They have to figure out where the venue is going to be and when it's available. Stuff like that."

"Right. You're right. It's just that it left me feeling like Holly wants them to get married more than Daniel does."

"Is that what Holly thinks, too?" asked Grayson.

I shook my head. "I don't think so. And she seems really happy. I'm going to just let it go. I'm sure everything is fine. We've met Daniel during a stressful time—he's just gotten engaged, and now he's heard someone he's close to was murdered. It can't be easy for him." I paused. "Hey, when you got up this morning, was Holly downstairs?"

"Nope. She came back in when I'd started the pancakes. She'd been out running an errand or something." Grayson noticed my frown. "Anything wrong?"

"No," I said quickly. "There's nothing wrong."

Chapter Seven

A few minutes later, Grayson and I walked into the large downtown library. The last time I was here, I'd done research in the South Carolina room. I had the feeling that's where I'd be most likely able to view maps of the Stone Fleet. Then I'd check out the newspaper archives, always a favorite activity of Grayson's, too, to find out more about Bianca's stance and those voicing opposition to her. So we headed upstairs to the second floor. As before, there were tables for research and the walls were lined with glass display cases of various artifacts.

I was glad to see a librarian I'd worked with from my previous visit. Meredith recognized me too and came over to say hi. She asked me how things were going at the Whitby library, and we chatted for a few minutes.

"Is Warner still coming in?" I asked. He was an amateur relic hunter I'd met during my last visit.

"Are you kidding?" asked Meredith with a snort. "He's here all the time. He's always looking at the Sanbourne maps to find likely spots for relics." She gave me a curious look. "What are you researching this time?"

Then I said, "I'm interested in finding out more information on the Stone Fleet. Could you help me get my hands on a map?"

The map was in a restricted area, full of file cabinets and bookshelves. Meredith led us over there, then snapped her fingers. "Hey, if you're interested in the Stone Fleet, you should come to the community meeting tomorrow. You'll be able to hear the different sides in favor and against the sand replenishment project."

"Thanks, we'll be sure to make that," I said. "What time is the meeting?"

"Lunchtime. Pretty sure it's right at noon, but you'll want to double-check me. I was interested in sticking my head in too, since that's when I take my lunch. It should be pretty animated. But quieter now that Bianca Donovan won't be there." She frowned. "You heard about that, didn't you?"

I nodded, not wanting to get into just how I'd heard about it.

"There's going to be another guy there to talk up the preservation of the Stone Fleet. His name is Nolan. I've never seen him on the same side as Dr. Donovan before, so that's worth coming right there."

"We'll try to make it, for sure," I said.

Meredith said, "And since you're a book nerd like me, you might be interested to know that Herman Melville immortalized the Stone Fleet in one of his poems."

Grayson said, "Herman Melville? Didn't he write *Moby Dick*?"

"The very one."

I said, "That's very cool. The guy was clearly really into ships, wasn't he? The Pequod was practically a character in *Moby Dick*."

Meredith nodded. "Interestingly enough, the Stone Fleet were *also* whaling ships. Retired, of course."

"So clearly really into *whaling* ships, then," said Grayson. "I'll have to look the poem up on my phone."

Meredith glanced through the glass door where a patron had just come in and seemed to wait for assistance. "I'd better run. Is there anything else I can help you find?"

"Can you just point the way to the newspaper archive? We'd like to read some of the local coverage regarding the controversy surrounding the Stone Fleet without hitting a paywall."

Meredith told us where to find it, then hurried away.

The map of the Stone Fleet that Meredith had produced was also accompanied by a newspaper clipping from 1862, which had a drawing of a ship sinking with other ships behind it.

I said, "I guess that was the most effective way to create a blockade back then."

Grayson was peering at the other materials that were filed with the map. "It says here they hoped to create sand shoals to prevent access to the harbor."

"Unsuccessfully, apparently," I said, pointing to another clipping.

Grayson said, "I'll pull the current newspapers from *The Charleston Post and Courier*."

I nodded absently, reading. Grayson returned minutes later with a stack of newspapers, all recent.

"The Second Stone Fleet isn't just in one particular area," I said. "It's scattered over a few hundred acres."

"So it wouldn't be a matter of protecting just a small area," said Grayson slowly.

"Right."

Grayson said, "To that point, one of the recent newspapers quotes Bianca extensively, saying she was trying to get the area designated as a historic district."

"Does the paper talk about the sand replenishment?"

Grayson skimmed the article, then shook his head. We were both quiet for another fifteen minutes, leafing through different pages. Then Grayson gave a low whistle.

"Okay, the beach renourishment project is fifteen million dollars."

I raised my eyebrows. "Wow. Okay, so it wasn't as if they needed just a small amount of sand. Declaring the area a historic district was going to prove a major obstacle to everyone who wanted that sand."

"Exactly. The article quotes developer Cooper Thornton as saying it was ridiculous to try and protect something that had been in the ocean for over a hundred and fifty years. And that the whaling ships that were part of the Stone Fleet were in terrible shape even in 1862, which was the whole reason the Union sank them."

"A fair point," I said. "What did Bianca say to that?"

Grayson was quiet as he read for a few moments. "She's talking about studying military strategy and shipwreck artifacts."

We continued researching for a few minutes. Grayson said, "It meant that the city council had to pay a good deal more money to the engineering firm to search for more sand."

"Does it talk at all about why it's so hard to find appropriate sand? I mean, it's a vast ocean. It seems like getting sand shouldn't be a big deal."

Grayson said, "It apparently has to match the sand that's already on the beach. It can't be too muddy, rocky, or have a lot of shells in it. It meant that the coastal engineering firm was probably going to have to extract sand from lots of different sites."

"And the state of the beach right now?"

"Well, some homeowners are using sandbags in front of their property. Erosion has been an issue because of storms and king tides," said Grayson.

I put away the Stone Fleet materials and helped Grayson skim through the newspapers. The main people against declaring the Stone Fleet as a national historic district were the developer, Cooper Harper, and the turtle team member, Sierra Barnett.

"Did you find the Herman Melville poem online?" I asked. "Meredith whetted my curiosity."

Grayson grinned at me. "I thought I remembered that you mentioned you weren't a huge Melville fan."

"Well, I got bogged down in all the chapters about harpoons. I was a huge fan of Queequeg, Melville's harpooner, though. And I rather liked *Billy Budd*, another Melville novel."

Grayson knit his brows as he searched on his phone for the poem. "Wasn't there a short story Melville wrote, too? I think I had to read it for school."

"Oh my gosh, yes. 'Bartleby, the Scrivener.' I mean, Melville wrote plenty of short stories, but I'm guessing you're talking about that one. Bartleby was rather obnoxious. He kept saying 'I prefer not to' the whole story."

Grayson said, "That's right." He peered down at his phone. "Here's the poem."

He skimmed it. "Sounds like Melville wasn't exactly happy about the ships being sunk for the blockade:

> *To scuttle them—a pirate deed—*
> *Sack them, and dismast;*
> *They sunk so slow, they died so hard,*
> *But gurgling dropped at last.*"

"To him, they were almost alive," I said.

Grayson nodded. "And at the end of the poem, he reminds the readers that the Union's mission with the Stone Fleet wasn't successful:

> *A failure, and complete,*
> *Was your Old Stone Fleet.*"

"Just one failed mission, though," I pointed out. "The Union ended up with the win in the end."

We took pictures with our phones of different maps, pictures, and articles. Then we let Meredith know we were done with the archival materials and took the newspapers back to the archive.

Grayson was thoughtful on the way back, and we were quiet for a few minutes. "So you're doing a little investigating, I'm guessing? For Holly?"

"For what it is, yes. It seemed to make her feel better that I was doing some research and poking around. She's worried about Daniel being a suspect."

Grayson asked, "Is that a legitimate concern?"

"Honestly, yes. I'm trying to put my first impressions of Daniel behind me to answer that question, although it's tough to do. But Daniel and Bianca have apparently been carping at each other in public over funding. And, of course, they're exes. So I'm guessing the police are at least going to check out the lead."

When we got back, some friends of Holly's had stopped by to visit. They were pulling out a blender to make frozen drinks. Grayson and I introduced ourselves, then Grayson grabbed a ball and Murphy, the golden retriever, happily followed him into the backyard. I was about to sneak out with him when Holly called out, "Come on, Ann, hang out with us."

I pasted a smile on my face and joined in. The introvert in me didn't feel up to it, but a little later I was glad I'd stayed put. They were a lot of fun, and I felt myself relaxing and joining in.

It ended up that the group ordered takeout a little later, and Grayson, who'd not had any of the frozen drink deliciousness, volunteered to go pick it up for everyone. Then they roped Grayson into staying. We ended up playing a board game Holly pulled out, accompanied by a lot of cheering and booing from the assorted winners and losers. By the time everyone dispersed, it was nearly midnight.

Holly gave a tremendous yawn. "Okay, that was an unexpected but totally fun evening. I'm going to crash. I don't remember when I was this tired."

Grayson and I waited for Holly to get out of earshot before cleaning up the mess in the kitchen. It wasn't too bad because everybody had been picking up after themselves. By the point everything was put away, I still felt sort of keyed up and not as tired as I should have been.

"Heading upstairs?" asked Grayson. He was yawning now, himself.

"I'm going to chill out down here for a little while. Too much excitement too late in the day," I said wryly.

Grayson gave me an understanding smile. He knew that I usually preface going to bed with reading a book for a couple of hours. "It was fun, though," he said.

"Oh definitely. I'll be up in a few."

The only problem then was that, instead of taking my book out to read, I started scrolling on my phone. That's definitely something I know better about. Scrolling through social media and the news isn't a relaxing thing to do at the end of the day.

Especially this time. There were local news reports about Bianca Donovan's death. And now it was obvious that she hadn't had a natural death, but had been strangled.

Chapter Eight

T he next morning, Grayson was reading the news story off my phone. He gave a low whistle. "I bet the cops are furious about that leak. There's no way they'd have wanted to release that information."

"I know. So, no natural death, obviously." I felt a chill go up my spine. "I wondered about that. I did see some red marks on her neck, but no bruising. I guess it had been too recent for bruising to show up."

"Somebody meant business," said Grayson.

We were downstairs. I was making eggs for everyone, since Holly had told us to make ourselves at home. And, for once, I was up earlier than Holly was.

"What's on the agenda for today?" asked Grayson.

"I think Holly's working this morning. We could head to the beach for a little while, then make that sand replenishment meeting back at the library." I sprinkled cheese into the eggs and kept scrambling. "Then there's that gallery show tonight that's going to feature Daniel's work."

"Sounds good," said Grayson.

Holly hurried into the kitchen. "I don't know how I managed to sleep through two alarms. I've got a virtual meeting in five minutes."

"Here, have some eggs." I scooped some out on a plate. "I'll bring your coffee in there. Milk and sugar, right?"

"Thank you," said Holly. "Too much fun last night with the girls." She hurried back out again, carrying the plate to a desk in her living room.

Thirty minutes later, Grayson and I tiptoed out the door and headed to the beach. The ocean was still warm, and it was blissfully quiet out there, mostly because school had already started back and it was a Monday morning. It was nearly high tide and Grayson and I did some body surfing until the water got too rough and shoved us both into the sand. Then we climbed out onto the beach and our towels, the warm sun drying the salty water off us. For the first time since getting to Charleston, I felt totally relaxed.

After we'd dried off, we set out for a walk on the beach. There was a dad flying a colorful kite for his amazed toddler, the wind whipping the kite around. Sand pipers were hunting and pecking for food at the water's edge. We walked for over a mile, hand in hand, past homes and hotels.

We gave ourselves enough time to get back, get cleaned up, grab a sandwich, and wave bye to Holly, who appeared stuck in virtual meeting Hades before heading out the door and back to the library.

By the time we reached the multipurpose room at the library, we were surprised to see most of the seats were full. We found the last two chairs together near the back of the room.

"Interesting mix of people here," said Grayson in a low voice.

It was. There were people who looked like they'd just stepped off the golf course, a group of people with turtle shirts on, a couple of very nerdy people in business dress, a tall man wearing a visor who seemed to know everyone in the room, and the police officer who'd responded to Bianca's murder. Morrow, I thought his name was.

Meredith, the librarian, slipped in right before the meeting started, lunch in hand. She waved in greeting to Grayson and me before standing in the back of the room to watch the proceedings.

I'd originally thought it might be a poor way to spend a lunch break, but as soon as the meeting kicked off, I saw it was a lot more animated than I'd expected. Grayson and I kept giving each other surprised looks as various people went up to support or speak out against the sand replenishment project. The sea turtle volunteers were especially persuasive, speaking about the need for more sand at Isle of Palms to support nesting. The tall man with the visor introduced himself as Cooper Thornton and spoke eloquently about how a planned development and all the jobs associated with its creation would be jeopardized if the beach wasn't replenished.

Grayson leaned over, "That's one of the guys in the article in the paper. The developer."

I nodded. "He's also a friend of Daniel's."

Then a man in his forties with a rugged build stood up. He had dark hair streaked with silver and was wearing cargo pants, a well-worn shirt, and sturdy hiking boots. He identified himself as Nolan Harper.

"That's the amateur archaeologist," I whispered.

Nolan spoke passionately for about twenty minutes about the need to protect history, the importance of the Stone Fleet, and the artifacts archaeologists hoped to find at the site. Although he seemed to know a lot about the subject, his manner was abrasive and abrupt. It also felt as if he was being condescending to his audience.

Maybe because of Nolan's manner, the tone in the room shifted. There were a few angry questions from the crowd of people. Nolan took them without really even looking at the people asking them, instead directing his comments to the windows at the back of the room. Most everyone seemed focused on the fact that the historic preservation of something that had been rotting in the ocean for over a hundred years didn't make a lot of sense. That there were more pressing needs than artifacts. Nolan was prickly about this, and his air of condescension grew even more obvious.

After Nolan stopped speaking, people drew him aside as the library representative thanked everyone for attending. But when Lieutenant Morrow motioned Nolan over, he tightened his lips and headed straight for the back of the room—where Grayson and I were still sitting.

"Okay to hang out for a few minutes?" I said to Grayson in an undertone. "That's the cop who is handling the murder."

Grayson's eyes widened, and he nodded. We proceeded to take out our phones and pretend to be absorbed in them. The general chatter in the room made for excellent cover, too.

Morrow introduced himself, then started quietly asking Nolan about his relationship with Bianca Donovan.

"We had a business relationship. Strictly business," said Nolan, already sounding defensive and heated. "We were both archaeologists."

Morrow said, "From what I understand, you're not a professional archaeologist."

Nolan's voice was icy. "I'm an archaeology enthusiast. I spend many, many hours engrossed in writings, artifacts, and research. I'm fully qualified."

Morrow said, "Okay." His voice was dubious. "I hear you and Bianca Donovan didn't get along particularly well."

"Who's saying that? That's not true at all. We might have had some professional differences of opinion, but that's it."

Morrow said, "But you've just admitted you're not a professional. Dr. Donovan, on the other hand, was the state archaeologist. It seems to me that whatever she thought on a topic would be the final word."

"Dr. Donovan was someone who cared about hearing different opinions on a subject. She wasn't close-minded as so many people are." Nolan's tone seemed to suggest that Morrow might well be one of those narrow-minded individuals.

Morrow changed tack. "Where were you early Saturday morning?"

"Surely, you don't think I could be involved in Bianca's death," said Nolan in a huff.

"If you could please just answer the question," said Morrow.

There was a pause. "I was at home, participating in a conference call with different archaeology buffs from various locations."

"Got it. I'll need a list of the names of the other partici-pants."

Nolan hesitated for a moment. Grayson and I exchanged a discreet look.

Finally, Nolan said, "Come to think of it, the conference was later in the morning. *Early* in the morning, I was working on putting together a workshop for fellow archaeology enthu-siasts. I'll be presenting the workshop in October. Yesterday morning, I was coming up with the schedule of presenters."

"By yourself? No one else was at home with you?"

Nolan seethed, "I live alone. Or is that a crime in itself?"

"It's not a crime. It just makes it difficult to verify that you were where you say you were. I also looked up your address. It's within easy walking distance of Bianca Donovan's house."

"I tell you, I had nothing to do with her death!"

The chatter in the room was still loud, but more people were now looking at the back corner.

Morrow said in a calm voice, "I'm sensing some obstruction coming from you."

"I just can't believe you'd think I might have something to do with the death of a colleague, that's all. I'm not a violent per-son. And I certainly wouldn't harm a hair on Bianca Donovan's head. I had a lot of respect for her."

"Really?" asked Morrow. "Because from what I hear, you've had plenty of tiffs with Dr. Donovan. Public ones where she dis-agreed with your stance on various archaeology issues."

"It was nothing like that. Experts are allowed to disagree."

Morrow said, "Why don't you tell me a little about Dr. Donovan? Help me get a better idea of what she was like."

Nolan seemed to be picking his words carefully. "Well, she attended Stanford for a bachelor's degree in archeology. As a result of her schooling, she ended up with a master's degree in anthropology with a focus on historical archeology. Bianca was considered an expert on GIS mapping and stratigraphy."

Morrow cut in. "I'd like to hear more of your *personal* opinion of her."

More hesitation from Nolan. "She was passionate about her job," he intoned. Resentment was an undercurrent in his voice. "Bianca was proud of her accomplishments, as she should be, which is how I know so much about her background. She spoke of them often. Bianca was at the top of her field and wanted to stay that way. She wasn't welcoming to upcoming archaeologists."

"Not welcoming? In what way?"

Nolan said, "Just that she wanted her way or the highway. Bianca had to have everything the way she wanted it." The more he spoke about her, the more bitterness cropped up in his voice.

"I thought you said she was open to new ideas and different opinions on a subject. You said she wasn't close-minded."

Having his words thrown back at him seemed to throw Nolan for a loop. "I guess it was a little bit of both. Look, I've got other things to do today. Are we done?"

Morrow stood up. "For now. Please provide your phone number in case I need to speak with you later."

Nolan provided it to him, and Morrow walked out of the room. Before Grayson and I could follow, Nolan muttered in an irritated tone, "I guess you two heard all of that. You were listening in the whole time."

Chapter Nine

We turned around, putting our cell phones away. I said, "Sorry. I recognized Lieutenant Morrow and was curious to hear if there was any information on Dr. Donovan's murder." I introduced myself and explained my brief connection with Bianca. "We're just trying to find out more about what happened."

"Who is he?" asked Nolan, gesturing to Grayson.

"I'm a journalist."

Nolan brightened at this, seeming to assume he was a local reporter with the *Post and Courier*. "Look, if you're an investigative journalist, you need to be aware of a few things. I know that Morrow guy made it sound like I've got a good reason to get rid of Dr. Donovan, but he was totally out of line. The police always jump to conclusions instead of putting in the time it takes to figure out actual suspects."

Grayson, to his credit, didn't correct Nolan's misconception at all. He was very willing to play the role of an investigative journalist with the Charleston paper. "So you're saying you didn't have a beef with Dr. Donovan?"

"She was fine," said Nolan, waving his hand dismissively. "I didn't have any major gripes with her. We were on the same team, right? She and I were trying to look out for and protect historic sites. You need to look into the other folks who had much bigger problems with Bianca. Start out with those turtle people. They're fanatics."

Grayson and I must have appeared doubtful at this because Nolan immediately doubled-down. "You think I'm kidding? Those guys would totally murder someone if they thought they were endangering their sea turtles. They really wanted that beach restoration to happen. You heard them attacking me when I was talking a few minutes ago, right? That's nothing. They were practically foaming at the mouth when they were talking to Bianca."

Grayson took out his phone again, scrolling to his notes app. "Okay. Is there a particular member of the turtle protection group that stands out?"

"Yes. That Sierra woman. She's the most vocal and adamant of the group. She's the one you really need to be talking to." Nolan looked across the room and made a face. "Now I've got some of those rabble rousers heading my way again. Gotta go." He moved toward the door, then stopped and handed Grayson a business card. "In case you want to reach out to me for your story." Then he strode swiftly out the door.

Grayson grinned at me. "So now I work for the Charleston paper."

"As an investigative journalist, no less. Good for you!"

We walked out of the community room to the parking lot. There we were waylaid by none other than Lieutenant Morrow.

"I saw you in the meeting and thought I'd have a word," he said. He looked inquisitively at Grayson, who quickly introduced himself. Of course, Grayson had also verified my alibi for Saturday morning.

Morrow said, "I wanted to make sure you had my card in case you thought of anything pertaining to the scene."

I wasn't really following. "In what way?"

"Mostly if you remembered people nearby. Someone leaving, especially. Or people walking by."

I pocketed his business card. "Unfortunately, I was mostly focused on my upcoming meeting with Bianca. But if I think of anything, I'll definitely let you know." I paused. "I pulled up the news last night and saw that Bianca's death appears to be murder. Is that correct?"

Morrow pressed his lips together in irritation before giving a curt nod. "It's foul play."

I also wanted to see if I could get any sort of confirmation on time of death. "Do you have a good idea when she was murdered? I know she was still warm when I was checking her vitals."

"The medical examiner believes she must have died in the hour before you arrived."

I nodded. "The news was saying she was strangled."

"That's correct." He looked irritated again. "There was a leak from the station. Toxicology was negative. And now I have a question for you."

I nodded again.

"My understanding is that you were here mainly for pleasure and partly for a work-related meeting with Dr. Donovan. Why were you at a meeting on the local beach renourishment? As far as I'm aware, you don't have any beaches in the mountains of North Carolina."

Fair question. "I was curious," I said. "I read about Dr. Donovan's defense of the Stone Fleet and wanted to learn more. I'm a research librarian, and I guess it's hard for me to stop learning even when I'm on vacation."

I gave Morrow a cheerful smile, which was not returned.

"I want to make sure you both don't interfere with an ongoing police investigation. I understand being curious, but you have to realize that there's someone very dangerous out there. If you do hear anything, make sure to reach out. You've got my number."

With that, Morrow headed to his car.

Grayson drove us back to Holly's place.

"How did it go?" asked Holly.

"Interesting," I said. "I hadn't thought much about how historical events can still affect present-day decisions. But I should have. William Faulkner wrote, 'The past is never dead. It's not even past.'"

Holly said, "Especially here in Charleston. The past intervenes all the time. But then, it's a very old city. Did the meeting get out of hand at all? From what I've seen on the local news lately, it seemed like people were getting pretty riled up about the issue."

"I could tell there's a lot of passion on both sides of the Stone Fleet issue. With Bianca acting in an official capacity, she was probably bearing the brunt of everything negative at those public forums."

"Who spoke in favor of preserving the Stone Fleet?" asked Holly. "Was it that Nolan guy?"

Grayson and I nodded. "Although I didn't think he did a great job presenting the side of historic preservation," I added. "He was fairly patronizing to the audience. I don't think that went over too well with the group. The more he spoke, the more fired up people seemed to get."

"Were there a lot of people in attendance?" asked Holly.

"A lot more than I thought there'd be," I said. "I guess it's a hot topic."

Grayson added, "The cops were there, too. Or one of them, at least. We got warned off from poking around."

"Yes," I said wryly. "I guess he thought we were taking far too much of an interest in South Carolina history, considering we were from North Carolina and here for vacation."

"Speaking of vacation, what do y'all want to do the rest of the day?" asked Holly. "And it's okay to say you'd just like to relax and do nothing, especially since your trip has gone in a sort of dark direction."

Grayson considered the question, then said, "I probably should make a foray into my uncle's house."

I could tell by the diffident tone of his voice that it wasn't something he was particularly looking forward to. And Grayson, when he wasn't looking forward to something, tended to put it off as long as possible. "Do you want me to come with you? Help you sort things out?" I offered.

Grayson had already made inroads on a previous trip to Charleston. But he'd tackled some of the easier stuff then—the furniture and his uncle's clothes. The clothing was donated, along with some of the furniture, although I hadn't gotten the impression he'd finished either job. He'd taken a couple of chairs and an odd table or two back to his place in a truck he'd rented. The plan, according to Grayson, was to go through his uncle's memorabilia. And this was likely to be the hardest part. His uncle had never married, never had children. He'd also apparently served as the repository for all sorts of family heirlooms. Whenever a family member hadn't known what to do with a family Bible, a photo album full of unfamiliar faces, or various jewelry or artwork, they'd sent it to his uncle.

Grayson gave me a rueful look. "I have the feeling this is going to be a lot to go through. I wish my parents had taken more of an interest. Of course, I guess if they had, the memorabilia still would have ended up with me eventually."

I gave him a sympathetic hug. "I know that's an enormous job. And I know what it's like to serve as a family curator of sorts." I'd never known my father and my mother died when I was very young. My great-aunt had raised me and served as my entire family. And, like Grayson's uncle, she was the one who'd kept all the family history and keepsakes. When she died, she gave me her cottage and everything that had come with it.

Grayson's eyes widened. "You know, I've never really thought about that. Of course; you've been through this before, yourself. Except you had it even worse. You were still in school, right? How did you manage sorting through everything?"

I laughed. "Does it really look like I sorted through it all?"

Grayson considered this. "You know, I think of that cottage as Ann Beckett, through and through. The books, the keepsakes. How did you make that work?"

"Well, it took a little time."

Holly said, "I remember when your great-aunt died. It wasn't long after we graduated from college, was it?"

"Just six months. I was already in grad school, getting my master's in library science. Living with my aunt." I shook my head. "It seemed like my whole world was falling apart."

It was something I didn't talk about very often. It had been a really bleak time.

Holly looked over at Grayson. "When I heard about Ann's aunt, I came right over. I was going to give her a hand with the house since I hadn't found a job yet." She gave me a smile. "I think the first couple of days we just sat around, cried, and drank wine."

"Yeah, that's pretty much my recollection, too. But then we rallied, right? We started working on it."

Holly said, "Hey, that was all you. You were so freaking organized. No wonder you're so good at your job." She looked over at Grayson. "Really, she's the one you need to have go over to your uncle's house with you. Ann had a whole system."

"A method to my madness," I said wryly.

"Not madness at all. You were like, 'Okay. I have a small house. Let me prioritize.' And that's what you did. You knew you couldn't keep everything. You weren't looking to spend money on storage every month. I remember you found a few family heirlooms that you really wanted to keep, then you put those on display."

Grayson said, "That's actually a pretty helpful approach. That way you can set aside the most important things first. It gets easier from there."

"Right. Then you get rid of the easy things, like I was saying. I didn't need, want, nor could use my great aunt's clothes, so I donated them. Most of the furniture I kept because I was poor and needed it." I chuckled. "Still am poor, actually, and buying furniture hasn't been a priority."

"What about all the pictures and things? Weren't there a lot of pictures?" asked Grayson.

"That's where Ann was super-practical. She tossed any picture that had scenery in it or people she didn't know. There were pictures of her great-aunt and her mom when they were young and Ann digitized them," said Holly.

"That sounds fancier than what I actually did, which was to take photos of the pictures. I didn't end up with the best quality, but I can see them on my computer whenever I want to pull them up. I tossed the originals. There were tons of albums."

Grayson said, "What I'm really curious to hear is how you handled your great-aunt's books."

Holly and I grinned at each other. "Okay, that was a different story. I have a hard time giving away books. I did find some were duplicates of titles I already owned, so those were easy to weed out. But I kept most of the rest. I've been reading them, too. There's some good stuff in there. Sometimes it's nice to read older books. It's like going back in a time machine."

Grayson said, "Well, you've inspired me. But I think I'm going to make this trip to my uncle's solo. Thanks for the offer though, Ann. I'd better assess what needs to be done and how much I think I can accomplish this afternoon. I'll check back in later."

After Grayson left, Holly tried to knock out all the work her meetings had generated for her before any other meetings popped up. I read my Pat Conroy book. I figured resting was probably not a bad idea. Daniel's gallery event sounded like something that might go on until late. After about an hour, Grayson came back in.

"How did it go?" I asked Grayson.

He gave me a rueful smile. "Well, I got some stuff done, anyway. The remainder of Uncle Bud's clothes were easy enough. I donated those right off the bat. Dropped them off at Goodwill on the way back over here."

"Hey, that's progress," I said. "Sometimes it's better to start off with a quick win, isn't it? That way you've already accomplished something and can feel good about delving into the minutiae."

"The little stuff is what's tripping me up every time. I did find his collection of old family photos and letters. That's going to take a while to wade through. A lot of it looked like it might be cool family memorabilia."

I said, "I'm sure your uncle would have loved that you found it interesting. Maybe that's why he left it to you? He felt like you'd appreciate it."

"Maybe." Grayson sounded doubtful. "Now I'm thinking that I should do what you were telling me—make photos of everything. There's no way I can get rid of it."

I knew Grayson had turned down my help before, but he really did seem like he was struggling with getting this done. "How about if I go over with you?"

"What? You mean right now? But this is your vacation."

"*Our* vacation. And you know how I love this kind of stuff. It's like doing archival work for the library. Besides, we'll be together. We don't have anything else pressing we need to be doing. And the work will be finished twice as fast with both of us snapping pictures and going through it. Unless you're already burned out on doing it today."

Grayson shook his head. "If you're really sure."

"Positive."

Chapter Ten

Just twenty minutes later, we were back at Grayson's uncle's house. It was a modest two-story structure with a classic Southern design, featuring a covered white porch supported by white columns. The front yard was neatly landscaped, with flowering bushes and a few shade trees.

"The yard looks great," I said in surprise.

Grayson grinned at me. "That's because I hired a yard service to take care of it. I wouldn't have been able to show up here and face the neighbors if I hadn't."

He drove us around down the paved driveway to a detached carport at the back of the house. Taking his keys, he let us into the house. We entered through the kitchen, which had vintage cabinetry, tiled countertops, and a cozy breakfast nook in a sunny corner. There were hardwood floors everywhere in the house, which all seemed to be in great shape.

"It's a beautiful house," I said, after Grayson gave me a quick tour.

"It is, isn't it? I think it'll sell pretty well, don't you?"

"I think it'll sell immediately," I said, meaning it. Not only was it in great shape, with a couple of updates in the bathrooms, it was in an excellent location.

Grayson looked cheerful at the prospect. "You're motivating me to get this tackled."

While he was feeling so motivated, I jumped right into the sorting. We took the photos and letters Grayson wanted to preserve into the kitchen, where there was plenty of natural light, and put them on the counter where the sunlight wasn't direct. We then took pictures, including the backs of photos sometimes too, since people's names were written on the back.

I knew both of Grayson's parents had passed away. They'd both been older when they'd had Grayson's sister, Carmen and Grayson. With Grayson's uncle dead, I wasn't sure what other family he had. "You could always email some distant relatives if you think they might find the pictures and letters interesting. I don't really have any family left, but I did find a distant cousin who seemed really appreciative of some things I sent along after my aunt died."

Grayson gave me a small smile. "That's true. None of our cousins were close to the family, though. I really never saw them, growing up. It might be tricky to find them." He paused. "Have you missed that kind of stuff? All the big family Thanksgivings and Christmases that we see on TV? Relatives gathered from near and far, singing carols and watching 'It's a Wonderful Life' while drinking cocoa?"

I raised an eyebrow. "Singing, watching TV, *and* drinking cocoa at the same time? Those sound like unusual gatherings."

He grinned. "Okay, maybe not all at the same time. But you know what I mean."

I shrugged. "When I was a kid, I did. But quiet holidays quickly got to feel normal. You and I should have a big Friendsgiving this year. Invite a bunch of people. Maybe we do it right before or right after the holiday."

"You're on," said Grayson, sounding pleased at this. We dove back into the sorting and picture taking, spending a couple of hours and knocking most of it out. Then we drove back to Holly's to put our feet up before going out again for Daniel's gallery event.

That night, we got dressed up and headed out with Holly. Daniel was going early to make sure everything was set up. Holly parked us in a parking deck and then we walked to an old mill that had been converted into a gallery. A sign out front gave the theme of the show as "Expressions Unveiled." Daniel was listed on the sign as this year's organizer, who'd spearheaded the annual showcase. The space had a lot of atmosphere, with its exposed brick walls, large arched windows, and original wooden beams. As we walked further into the building, we heard a string quartet playing in one corner.

Daniel was one of fifteen artists who were showing their work that night. The artists all seemed to be in different media. There was stunning black-and-white photography showing everyday Charleston with a surreal twist, wooden sculptures depicting human forms and emotions, and a mixed media exhibit combining paper, fabric, and found objects.

Daniel greeted Holly with a quick kiss and smiled at Grayson and me. He seemed to keep an eye on the door, though, and I had the feeling he might disappear at a moment's notice.

Holly looked pleased as punch at being there and proud of Daniel, to boot. "Why don't you walk us over to your work?" she asked him. "Maybe you can explain some of the artwork to us?"

A frown of displeasure streaked across Daniel's features. I had the feeling he didn't like the idea of explaining art. He proved me right a moment later when he asked, "Explain it?"

Holly flushed. "It's not like it *needs* any explanation, of course. I meant maybe you could tell us what you were thinking when you created the work."

I wasn't sure that would make Daniel less irritated, and it didn't seem to. But this time he didn't say anything out loud, just muttered under his breath as he led us over to his work.

I could see why Holly thought explanations might be in order. One of his paintings seemed to be a dreamscape, with ethereal landscapes and distorted figures. Another was a psychedelic abstraction with swirling patterns and bright neon colors to make a bold composition. There was also a geometric abstraction of some kind with patterns and shapes arranged in non-linear formats.

Before Daniel could really properly introduce us to his work, explanations or not, he was called away by the gallery owner. He looked relieved to be leaving us, although Holly seemed deflated when he left.

Grayson cleared his throat. "Very powerful work," he offered.

"Yes," I hopped in. "The paintings introduce all sorts of feelings, don't they? They make me think they're portraying somebody's inner thoughts, fears, or desires."

Holly gave us a pleased smile. "That's exactly what I think, too."

Grayson took another crack at critiquing them. "There's a genuine sense of energy and movement in his paintings. They draw the eye in, don't they?"

"Yes, they do," agreed a pleasant voice behind us.

We turned to see the charismatic man from the library meeting we'd attended. He wore well-fitted jeans, a button-down shirt, and a pair of loafers.

Holly smiled at the man. "Hi, Cooper."

He reached out to give her a hug and a light kiss on the cheek. "Holly! Good to see you. Where's that genius fiancé of yours?"

"He's around here somewhere," said Holly lightly.

Sure enough, Daniel was next to us in seconds with a smile on his face. I remembered Daniel saying earlier that Cooper was a big supporter of the arts, both by donating money and by buying art. Maybe Daniel was hoping Cooper had a space for one of his works.

Cooper was slapping Daniel heartily on the back. "Daniel, my man! Great show tonight. Great show. Do you know, your art totally transcends the canvas."

Daniel gave him a rather obsequious smile. "I'm glad you like it."

"Like it? I love it. Going to buy one or two of them tonight for my place. I know exactly where I want to put them. I've got a sofa that would coordinate perfectly with one of them."

Daniel gave a rather pained smile. "Good, Cooper. Thank you." I could tell he didn't like the idea of art being an accessory for a sofa any more than he'd liked the idea of explaining his paintings.

Cooper continued prattling on. "That chiaroscuro technique you've employed—masterful! It's like you're inviting us into a realm where time itself is a malleable medium. And those nuanced brushstrokes of yours? Amazing. It's like your art engages with the viewer on a metaphysical level."

Grayson and I exchanged a look on the down-low. Cooper was either extremely knowledgeable about the arts, or he was using gobbledygook to make himself sound smart.

Daniel smirked. "Cooper, you sure have a way with words. That's high praise coming from an expert like you. You've always had a really discerning eye when it comes to art. Don't you think so, Holly?"

Holly quickly said, "For sure. It's nice to see someone of Cooper's stature appreciating and supporting the local arts scene."

They continued complimenting each other for several minutes, then Cooper said, "Tell me how things are going for you personally, Daniel. I'm looking forward to your engagement dinner." He affected a solemn expression. "Hey, I heard about Bianca Donovan. I'm so sorry about that. I know how close you were."

Holly had a tight smile on her face. Daniel nodded and said sadly, "I feel awful about it. Bianca had so much life ahead of her. I can't believe she was struck down in her prime like that." He gestured toward me. "Ann discovered Bianca, actually."

Cooper looked surprised, then appraising. "Is that so? That must have been awful for you. Were you a friend of Bianca's?"

"No, I was actually there for a business meeting with her."

"Oh, you're an archaeologist?" Cooper's brows knit together. I had the feeling he had fairly low regard for archaeologists.

"A librarian, actually. I was meeting with Bianca on a matter relating to historical preservation."

Cooper said, "And you found her inside her house?" He leaned in closer.

I nodded, resisting the urge to flinch at the memory. Every time the scene was brought to mind, it's like I was back there, finding Bianca.

"Let yourself in, did you?" Again, he gave me that appraising look. His voice held a hint of skepticism, as if he couldn't quite believe I'd taken such a bold step.

"That's right. After several minutes of doorbell ringing and pounding on the door." I didn't like how defensive I sounded. And I didn't like that I'd allowed myself to feel that way.

Cooper scrutinized me, as if trying to figure me out. He asked, "Were the news reports correct? Was she strangled?"

I answered coolly, not wanting to divulge more information than necessary. "I'm not a medical professional. I couldn't tell what was wrong."

Cooper's interest waned at my response, his focus shifting elsewhere. "Pity. The police have been chatting with me about her death," he remarked casually, as if discussing the weather. He glanced over at Daniel. "I'm guessing they've been talking to you, too."

Daniel gave a careless shrug, underscoring his indifference to the ongoing investigation. "They're probably talking to everybody."

Cooper rolled his eyes. "They must be desperate to find suspects. Of course, I didn't have a good alibi for them. Innocent people don't think like that. I don't get up in the morning with a plan for making sure my every move is documented by someone else. I was out inspecting a remote real estate property. No cameras or witnesses to prove it."

Holly said, "I guess Bianca's death is good news for your development project, though."

Daniel gave her a small frown, and Cooper looked a little surprised at her tone. "Well, I suppose it is, if you want to look at the bright side. And just about everything has a bright side, doesn't it? But I'm genuinely saddened by Bianca's death. The city has lost a valuable advocate for historical preservation. I highly respected her work as the state archaeologist and her dedication to preserving Charleston's history."

There was something practiced in his words, as if he were camera ready in case the press asked him about Bianca's death. But then, they probably had.

"Now, I'm not saying we weren't often on opposite sides of an issue. Naturally, my job is to develop property. That's just what I do. Bianca often wanted to preserve it. But I also saw my job as involving preservation, too."

I tilted my head to one side, and Cooper laughed. "You wouldn't think that, would you? It's true, though. Take the beach renourishment. That project preserves the beach, which provides a tremendous source of tourism revenue for the area. Bianca's budget for historical preservation would have dried up without that. Tourism is good for replenishing the government's coffers."

Daniel hopped in. "You're absolutely right. Great point."

Cooper continued. "Sometimes Bianca was a little too narrow-minded when it came to preservation. Take the Stone Fleet, for example. Bianca was taking things too far with that. The fleet was basically already destroyed. It had been underwater for one-hundred-and-fifty years. *Salt*water. Not exactly the right way to protect anything. And she was trying to get the remains of the second Stone Fleet placed on the National Registry of Historic Places, for heaven's sake. What's more, she didn't want to just preserve the wrecks, but the sand they lay on."

Daniel's head bobbed up and down in agreement. "It was ridiculous."

"It wasn't something that could be turned into an exhibit," said Cooper. "Nobody could go out there to visit it and learn anything. On the other hand, the sand replenishment was there to help all sorts of people."

Cooper must have noticed that I considered that a stretch because he said insistently, "It's true. Think of the folks whose jobs depend on beach tourism. And the turtle people who need to make the beach better for the sea turtles to nest and lay eggs. What about the residents who live along the coast?"

Holly added, "And your own project, of course. The hotel on the inlet."

Cooper gave a hearty laugh. Daniel was flushed with irritation.

"All right, Holly, I'll give you that," said Cooper. "It's going to benefit me, too. But why not? I've worked hard to get that hotel started. It's going to be a fantastic place for families to stay." He paused. "I'm not going to say I'm not sorry that Bianca and I didn't get along better when she was alive. We had a few heated discussions during community meetings and conferences on the city's future. But we respected each other's passion and commitment to Charleston."

Holly said, "Is there somebody you can think of who Bianca was having issues with? Somebody who might have wanted to do this to her?"

Cooper wagged a finger at her. "Trying to steer the police away from your fiancé, are you? Who can blame you? Sure, there were plenty of people on Bianca's bad side. Eleanor Johnson was one of them."

Eleanor was the older lady who spoke with me outside Bianca's house after I found Bianca's body.

Cooper said, "I know Eleanor was harassing Bianca all the time. Wouldn't leave her alone. Anytime there was any sort of community forum, Eleanor was there stalking Bianca."

Grayson cleared his throat. "What was Eleanor upset about?" Grayson already knew the answer to that from me, but I appreciated his looking for Cooper's take on it.

Cooper looked surprised to see Grayson, as if he'd forgotten he was there. "Well, Bianca wanted to turn some of Eleanor's family land into public historic property."

"And Eleanor wanted to keep the land in the family?" asked Grayson.

"You'd think so, wouldn't you? If you were to talk to Eleanor Johnson for more than just a couple of minutes, you'd hear all kinds of stories praising her family to the heavens. Actually, it's her *husband's* family, but whatever."

I asked, "But Eleanor didn't actually want to keep the land in the family?"

"Not a bit. She reached out to me last year to investigate developing part of the property, on the outskirts of it. Eleanor wanted me to consider building a few homes there. Or maybe *more* than a few homes. Let's just say she was open to ideas. They're a family that loves their local status and influence. However, they're a little low on funds."

"What was the historical significance of the property?" asked Grayson.

Daniel was looking bored with the conversation. His gaze strayed across the room where a couple was studying one of his paintings and pointing out various aspects of it.

Cooper said, "Oh, there was definitely some historical relevance. Because of the Johnson property's elevation and proximity to water, it was a strategic military post for observing and controlling movements in the area."

Daniel lifted a brow. "You've been following the news on it."

"Yep," said Cooper cheerfully. "I'm a Revolutionary War buff. Why not, right? Everybody needs a hobby."

Grayson asked, "Was that just conjecture? Or were there documents supporting it?"

"Good question! Bianca had actually dug up maps from that era and correspondence between military leaders. Some preliminary excavations revealed a cache of military artifacts, too."

"Why would Eleanor have even allowed archaeologists onto her property? It seems that would have been a good way to shut down even the idea that there could be something there," I said.

"I asked Eleanor the same thing," said Cooper. "She told me that Bianca had gotten in touch with her husband for permission. He's generally clueless, so Bianca was smart to reach out to him instead of Eleanor. Then, when her team was on her property, she found those artifacts."

Daniel was looking across the room again.

"What kinds of artifacts?" asked Grayson curiously.

"Musket balls, uniform buttons, things of that nature. Interesting stuff. Anyway, if Bianca had gotten her way, that land would be part of a public museum and preserved. Eleanor was furious about that. I overheard Bianca telling Eleanor to back off and stop calling her and dropping by her house all the time. Eleanor was seriously harassing her."

Before I could ask more about Eleanor, a man in a suit came up to pull Cooper into a conversation. Daniel bounded away to talk with other guests about his work. Soon he was laughing, shaking hands, and acting like the life of the party.

Holly said wryly, "I thought artists were supposed to be introverted."

"I guess it helps to be extroverted if you're trying to sell your work," I said with a smile.

We made the rounds, seeing all the different types of art on display. It turned out to be a fun evening. There were lots of people there, the music changed out to a jazz band, and there were delicious food and drinks. It ended up being another late night, although Grayson, Holly, and I left a lot earlier than Daniel did.

On the way back, Holly said, "You know, we've been hearing a lot about the turtle team folks. The ones who were fighting Bianca on the sand replenishment. Maybe we need to make a plan to talk to one or more of them." She made a face. "Sorry, I guess I'm obsessed. I really just don't want Daniel to continue being a suspect."

"I totally understand that. I heard someone named Sierra was sort of the spokesperson of the group," I said. "Do you know the best way to speak with her?"

"I actually know Sierra, myself. Just a little, I mean. When she's not volunteering with the turtles, she's actually a great masseuse. She owns her own mobile massage business, and my mom and dad have given me gift cards for her from time to time. Aside from booking a massage, which would be taking things a little far, tomorrow is Tuesday and I know the turtle team hosts Tuesday turtle walks. It's going to mean an early start, though."

"That's convenient," said Grayson. "What are the turtle walks?"

"It's when the volunteers walk the beach at dawn to look for sea turtle footprints. If they find a nest, they post a loggerhead turtle nesting sign and cordon off the area to protect the nest. They invite the public to tag along for those."

"And you think Sierra is likely to be there?" I asked.

"Almost definitely. She's great, but just a heads-up that she can be pretty garrulous when she gets talking." Holly paused thoughtfully. "Maybe I need to reach out to her soon for another massage now that I'm engaged. Planning a wedding can mean a lot of stress."

Holly said she had a couple of errands to run the next morning before work, so Grayson and I made plans to head out to the Isle of Palms to join the turtle walk.

Chapter Eleven

Meeting up at six a.m. meant setting a particularly early alarm. Early enough that I pulled the bedspread over my head in denial that it was actually morning. It didn't take long, though, for us to get up, get ready, and head out the door with granola bar breakfasts to join the group.

The sun was peaking up over the horizon when we joined in. It was still muggy outside, but the wind was strong, which made it feel a lot cooler than it was. There were five tagalongs, two volunteers, and a ranger there. Despite the early hour, no one looked sleepy when the ranger spoke. She explained how the hatchlings worked together to push through the sand and reach the surface. Apparently, it took sixty days for the hatchlings to leave the nest and hurry off to the ocean in the night toward the brightest light, which should be the ocean if the residents have been good about turning off their outside lights. The ranger introduced the two volunteers, one of whom was indeed Sierra Barnett. She was an athletic woman with sandy-blonde hair tied in a loose ponytail.

The ranger also asked us to pick up litter, fill in any holes, and knock down any sandcastles that might present an impediment to the hatchlings. We all found plenty to do as we walked. It was especially cool to see the nests and inspect them with the others in the group.

At the end of the walk, the others were heading off to their cars. I sidled up to Sierra and introduced myself. "I'm a friend of Holly Walsh. She mentioned what a great masseuse you are."

Although Holly had talked about how chatty Sierra was, that wasn't really in evidence right then. In fact, Sierra looked distracted—almost like she was in a fog. She thanked Grayson and me for coming on the walk. Then she said with a short laugh, "Sorry if I'm a little out of it right now. It's been a rough week. I think I need a massage, myself." She paused. "Holly knew Bianca Donovan, didn't she?"

"I think they might have been acquainted, but she didn't know her well." I wasn't actually sure Holly had met Bianca at all. The way she was talking, she only really knew who she was because of Daniel and Bianca being featured in the local news.

Sierra said in a bitter voice, "Yeah, I thought Bianca and I were just acquaintances, too. But the police have been trying to drag me into it all. All I'm trying to do is help out the sea turtles, you know?"

Grayson asked, "Why do you think the police are focusing on you?"

Sierra gave him a wry look. "Probably because I get too wound up about this stuff. I'm always shooting my mouth off in public meetings or in front of a camera. But that's just because I care. I mean, yes, Bianca and I were on other sides of the beach replenishment. She couldn't understand where I was coming from and I couldn't understand her position, either. Bianca acted like she cared more about stuff that's already rotting away in the ocean than living, breathing things. I couldn't figure it out."

I said, "Were you able to give the police an alibi for Saturday?"

"Nope. Usually I could, though. I'm ordinarily working on a Saturday morning, but I didn't have any early appointments, so I just slept in. I'd been staying up late the last few nights before Saturday and was totally knocked off my sleep schedule. Naturally, I had to pick a morning to sleep in when I needed an alibi."

"That's nice that you have your own business, though. It's got to be great to set your own schedule," said Grayson.

"Oh, it definitely is. I used to work for a massage parlor, but I hated the way they'd take most of what I earned. I decided to set up shop myself. So I got a loan and created a mobile massage parlor." She looked across the beach. "I love being part of the turtle team in my spare time, though. It just got frustrating when I knew the beach needed renourishment and the whole process was getting stonewalled by the state."

Grayson said, "I understand that there's a lot to consider with choosing sand for replenishment."

"That's right. If the sand is too compacted, it can make it tough for sea turtles to nest. Or if the sand is really different from what's already on the beach, it can affect everything: incubation temperature, the moisture in the nests, stuff like that. It's tricky. But the sand that was by the Stone Fleet was supposed to be a good match. That's why it was so frustrating."

"What was it like to deal with Bianca?" I asked.

Sierra sighed. "You know, I didn't have to interact with her as much as the cops think. When I did, I was always cordial.

I was simply trying to explain to her how the beach replenishment would help the turtles. I guess Bianca thought she was doing the right thing. She was trying to protect history. But like I said, I couldn't understand how she could care so much about something from the past and want to protect it more than animals. To answer your question, though, she seemed very educated and professional."

"It sounds like she wasn't too bad to work with," said Grayson.

Sierra frowned. "That's not really the case, though. The problem with Bianca is that she didn't listen. Not to me, not to anybody. She'd nod her head, but I never got the impression that she was actually listening or even cared." She gave a short laugh. "I heard her tell somebody after a community meeting that I was an extremist."

"Was Bianca often like that? Sort of condescending?" I asked.

"Exactly like that. Mostly behind your back, though. I'm no extremist—I'm just passionate about what I do, and I feel like I'm making a difference. I have all these amazing memories from when I was a kid and out on the beach with my mom. We'd always keep an eye out for the turtles. If she were still alive, she'd be so excited about what I do. The payoff is the number of successful hatches and emergences from the nests. And I've made some lifelong friends with the Island Turtle Team. We're almost like a family."

"Sounds like a great group," I said.

"Sure is. And it helps me relax a little with all this stress going on. I mean, owning your own business is stressful enough without having the cops question you about a murder."

Grayson said, "Can you think of somebody else who Bianca might have made upset? Somebody else who might have wanted to harm her?"

"Good idea," said Sierra, jabbing a finger at him. "I need to get the heat off myself. Sure, there are probably a couple of people. That awful guy she used to date, for one. Daniel, I think his name is."

Grayson and I glanced at each other. "What made him so awful?" I asked.

"I don't even know the guy, but you can tell he made her furious at the drop of a hat. He'd come along with her to different community forums or council meetings and they'd end up arguing over ridiculous stuff like whether the room was hot or cold. He was just like poison for her."

I said, "I understood the two of them had broken up."

Sierra shrugged. "Maybe they had, but it sure seemed like they were still spending a lot of time together to me. I saw them talking to each other just a week ago. I figured it was just one of those on again/off again relationships." She paused. "Then there was that other archaeologist guy. Nolan. He was always giving Bianca a hard time. He acted like he knew more than she did, and she had all kinds of advanced degrees."

Sierra then glanced across at the park ranger, who seemed to be packing up. "Good talking to you, but I want to speak with the ranger for a few minutes before she heads out. And I've got to get my walk in, too. Thanks for coming out this morning."

Grayson and I walked back to the car. "What did you make of all that?" asked Grayson as he started up the car.

"Sierra seemed pretty indignant at the police attention. But then, everybody has always said how passionate she is about protecting the turtles. She makes a good spokesperson for the group."

Grayson said, "I could tell when she was talking how she didn't understand Bianca's position at all. How Bianca seemed more worried about history than living creatures."

"Right. But Sierra also said that she thought Bianca was very professional"

"Except when she was calling her an extremist," said Grayson dryly.

"Maybe the truth falls somewhere in-between. Maybe Sierra isn't exactly an extremist, but she could carry things too far and act out in the heat of the moment."

Grayson asked, "Do we have any more likely suspects?"

I considered this. "Well, there's Daniel. I hate to include him on the list, though. Poor Holly."

"I have to admit that I haven't gotten the best impression of the guy, either. What do you think Holly sees in him? She's usually so levelheaded."

"Daniel can definitely be charming when he wants to be. We saw that last night."

"When he was speaking with that developer," said Grayson with a small eye-roll.

"True. But probably also with Holly much of the time. And he's certainly talented, even if some of his art isn't totally up my alley. The problem is that he apparently had this really volatile relationship with Bianca Donovan, even in the public eye. Maybe he lost control and killed her."

Grayson said, "At her house? Early in the morning? Do you think he was cheating on Holly?"

"Maybe he went over to Bianca's house to speak with her about allocations for art instead of archaeology. We've heard that was something that was a source of contention between the two of them." I shrugged. "I don't know. I really don't want to think he had anything to do with it at all. I just want Holly to be happy."

Grayson said, "How about that other archaeologist? Nolan? The guy we saw speaking at the library. He seemed kind of pompous to me. And we keep hearing that he and Bianca didn't get along well."

"Right. Apparently, she wasn't very impressed with Nolan's approach to archeology. From what I saw on Sunday, he didn't act like he enjoyed being questioned by the audience. I thought that triggered him to be condescending to people. Maybe he thought Bianca was looking down on him and couldn't take it anymore. Or maybe it wasn't even something that was actually planned out—he could have gone over to speak with her about the Stone Fleet, gotten angry, and just lashed out at her."

Grayson nodded. "Strangulation seems like a spur-of-the-moment crime to me. Who else do we have?"

"Well, there's Eleanor Johnson. She's the lady I met outside of Bianca's house."

"Right," said Grayson. "You said she was trying to protect her family's land."

"That's what it sounded like at the time. Now we know it's technically her husband's family's land. Although she's just as possessive of it."

Grayson nodded. "Then, at the gallery opening, Cooper said she actually was interested in selling the land and having him look at developing it."

"That's right. At least, developing part of the family property. But that was some of what the state of South Carolina wanted to protect and open to the public as a historic site."

Grayson said, "That sure sounds like a motive for murder to me."

"Although I'm sure someone else will take up the cause to claim the Johnson property for historic purposes. So it seems a little pointless."

Grayson offered, "But if we're thinking it was a heat-of-the-moment crime, it could fit. Eleanor might have been frustrated and angry enough with Bianca that she just snapped for a minute." He paused. "You did say she was elderly though, right? And Bianca was a young woman."

I shrugged. "Eleanor was older, but definitely seemed strong and able. The kind of person who probably has worked in her garden every day of her life. I wouldn't put anything past her."

We arrived back at Holly's house and found her inside, a determined look on her face. "When I was out running my errands, I ended up driving by Bianca's house. I stopped for a minute to talk to one of her neighbors who was out pulling weeds."

I'd known from our college days that Holly could be like a dog with a bone when she got something into her mind. She was now totally focused on clearing Daniel's name. Holly had mentioned her family hadn't exactly embraced Daniel and that it would be worse if they realized he was a suspect in a murder case. "What did you find out?" I asked.

"Her neighbor said she'd told the police there'd been a silver vehicle outside Bianca's house that morning. She couldn't remember what kind of vehicle it was until I pulled up a picture online of the make and model of Sierra's car. She said that was it."

I frowned. "Okay. Not the massage business van? I thought that was the vehicle you'd associate with Sierra, since you used her mobile massage business.

"Most of the time she *was* in the van. But a couple of times, she came in her personal car when I said I just wanted a chair massage. It saved her the trouble of lugging everything out. But I totally remember what the car looked like. It had turtle bumper stickers all over it."

"Wow," I said slowly. "So Sierra was over at Bianca's house the morning she died?"

Holly was putting a pair of sandals on. "I want to have a word with Sierra about that. She's still at the beach, right?"

I exchanged a look with Grayson. "Why not just call the police and have them handle it?"

"And have them just tell me to mind my own business? No way. Come on—there's three of us and only one of her. Let's head back out to the beach."

There was no stopping Holly in that frame of mind. We hopped into her car and headed back to the beach again. I talked about the turtle walk that morning and what we'd seen, but I could tell Holly was completely distracted. We fell into silence as she drove, faster than usual, toward the beach.

We found a place to park, then walked onto the beach. It was still very quiet there, although it was picking up. I could see some dog walkers in the distance.

"She said she was planning on taking a walk," Grayson said. "But she didn't say what direction she was going in."

Holly said, "Let's just wait here, then. I saw her car in the parking lot. She'll come back eventually." She threw down a couple of towels that she kept in her trunk and had retrieved when we exited the car.

One of the dog walkers came closer. The dog was off-leash, which was allowed until nine in the morning. The golden retriever was joyfully chasing seagulls and sandpipers, romping in the waves, and generally loving life. His owner was trailing behind at a slower pace, pausing sometimes to stretch, and look at the ocean.

Then the dog's behavior changed. He started backing up and barking, almost pointing to a spot in the sand at the water's edge, where a limp form moved listlessly with the waves.

"Did something wash ashore?" Holly asked, squinting into the rising sun.

I stood up slowly, shielding my eyes from the sun with my hand. "It looks like something pretty big."

"Sometimes porpoises wash up. It's awful when they do."

I said quietly, "I think it's a person. The body of a person."

Right at that moment, the dog walker started screaming.

Chapter Twelve

We hurried down toward the body on the beach. Grayson was already calling the police as we went. The dog walker corralled her golden retriever with some difficulty, pulling him back from the scene. Holly and Grayson stayed back as I searched for a pulse I couldn't find. It was Sierra Barnett. I noticed marks on her wrists and arms, as if she might have been restrained or held down against her will.

Holly's teeth were chattering as if she was freezing. "What do we do?" she asked. "Won't she wash away if we don't pull her in?"

Grayson had wrapped up his call with the police and searched online. "The tide is coming in, so she shouldn't wash out to sea."

"We should stand back and try to protect the scene by keeping anyone from getting too close," I said.

Holly nodded. "It's going to be crowded out here soon."

I took a few pictures of the area before the tide covered them up. I wasn't sure if the footprints I saw would help the police or not.

Fortunately, the cops came quickly, hustling us up toward the dunes and out of the way. Holly had called Daniel. Her voice was shaking as she spoke to him. "We came down to the beach and found Sierra dead. In the water. Can you come? I really need you." There was a pause while she listened to whatever Daniel was saying. "Can't you do that later? Okay. See you in a minute."

Sirens were already approaching. Holly threw a towel back down on the sand and sat abruptly, like her legs didn't want to hold her up any longer. "I can't believe this. I feel awful—I thought Sierra killed Bianca. But now the killer got her, too." She looked at us. "Right? Is that what you think, Ann?"

I said slowly, "From the marks I saw on her arms and wrists, it looked like somebody held her down."

"What is going on?" said Holly to herself. "At least we know Daniel wasn't here."

But Daniel arrived just a few minutes after the police. Grayson and I exchanged a glance. Wherever he'd been, it hadn't been very far away.

He gave Holly a quick hug, looking broodingly across the sand at the activity on the beach. "You okay?" he asked gruffly. Holly nodded, although she definitely looked a lot less than okay.

The police had done their best to cordon off the area with crime scene tape and stakes, despite the incoming tide. There were more people hanging around the area. Some officers were taking photos from various angles. Another was talking to the dog walker who'd calmed down, even if her dog had not. I saw Detective Morrow arrive on the scene, speak with the other police officers, and then talk on the phone and to the dog walker for a moment. Then he headed in our direction.

He reintroduced himself, then pulled out a small notebook. "How is it that all of you ended up here this morning?" It sounded like a casual question, but there was an undercurrent that suggested it wasn't.

Daniel quickly raised his hands defensively. "I wasn't here. I just drove up because my girlfriend called me."

Fiancée, I thought.

Morrow might have thought the same thing because he pressed his lips together for a moment. "What were you doing until now?"

Daniel ran a hand through his hair. His face was pale and taut and the defensiveness was now coming clearly through his voice. "I was at my place."

"Could you provide a little more information than that?"

Daniel said, "What kind of timeframe are you talking about?"

Morrow looked at Grayson and me. "The last hour and a half," I said.

Daniel went completely in the opposite direction with sharing information. "Well, my alarm went off around seven. I showered, started a load of laundry, then ate breakfast. I had bacon, eggs, and hash browns. Once I'd finished eating, I got the phone call from Holly. I drove over here as quickly as I could." He looked defensive again. "Within the speed limit, of course."

Morrow nodded and jotted down a few notes, as if Daniel's retelling was more informative than it actually was. "Got it." The detective tapped his pen against the notepad. "I've been wanting to catch back up with you, anyway. You know, I tried to contact you yesterday several times. I called, left messages. Texted. It sure seemed like you were avoiding me."

"I was busy yesterday—getting ready for a show. Ask anybody."

"At least I've got you now. Want to speak with me for a few minutes in private?"

Daniel threw his arm around Holly. "Whatever you need to say to me, you can say in front of Holly."

Holly gave a weak smile.

Morrow bared his teeth in a grin. "Okay. The thing is, Mr. Reynolds, I've been talking to a bunch of folks about Bianca Donovan. What people have been telling me is that you had quite a relationship with Dr. Donovan."

"*Past* relationship," said Daniel coldly. His arm tightened around Holly's shoulders.

"Is the past ever really past?" asked Morrow, echoing my quoting of Faulkner earlier. "Maybe not. From what I've heard, you and she always seemed to meet up at different venues and events."

"Accidentally."

"Sure," said Morrow. "Accidentally. The problem that I have, though, is that these meetings, accidental or not, were never very friendly. The two of you would argue."

"Bicker. We'd bicker."

Morrow tilted his head to one side, his eyes hidden behind dark sunglasses. "Well, I guess that's a matter of opinion. From what I heard, you both made very public scenes. And you weren't shy about expressing your point of view, especially when it clashed with hers."

"It's a free country," said Daniel with a shrug. His eyes narrowed. "We were perfectly pleasant to each other. Whoever says differently is lying. In fact, I briefly caught up with Bianca recently. She told me Eleanor Johnson was driving her crazy. Maybe you should be checking *her* out."

Morrow gazed back at Daniel with a non-committal look. "What else did Dr. Donovan say about Mrs. Johnson?"

"Oh, she'd heard rumors that Eleanor and her family were in a tough financial position. That they'd been living above their means for years, and it was finally catching up with them. They wanted to sell a parcel of land. That's what it all was coming down to—money. And the only thing standing in the way of Eleanor selling land was Bianca." Daniel gave a short laugh. "It's obvious, isn't it? She was desperate to get rid of Bianca so she could develop that land."

Morrow scrawled another note on the pad. "Okay. Tell me a little about Sierra Barnett. What do you know about her?"

Daniel pulled his arm away from Holly, the better to gesticulate. "Nothing, man. I don't know anything about Sierra Barnett. All I know is what everybody else knows about her from watching the local news. She was one of those turtle preservation people. I do know that Bianca mentioned that Sierra was making her frustrated."

"Right," said Morrow. "Because of the sand replenishment issue.

"She wouldn't leave it alone. Even worse, Bianca said Sierra was her masseuse. And she was apparently pretty good at her job. So good that Bianca wasn't looking for anyone to replace her, even though Sierra wouldn't shut up about the turtles."

This was news to me. Sierra never mentioned that Bianca was a client. Of course, she'd said she'd slept in on Saturday morning when Bianca's neighbor told Holly she'd seen her silver car parked outside.

More people were coming down from the road to survey the beach. They couldn't completely see what was going on near the water's edge, so they were getting as close as possible. One person who was passing by us mentioned wondering if there were riptides and drownings.

Morrow ignored everyone. "You're saying that there are a couple of other people who might have wished Bianca Donovan harm. And you're also saying Sierra was one of them. But Sierra was the victim today."

"Like I said, I don't know anything about Sierra. You were asking me about people who might have been having issues with Bianca, and she was one of them."

Morrow tapped his pen on the notepad again. "See, I don't think you're being all that forthcoming about Bianca. I just have too many witnesses who say you had an acrimonious relationship with her. And the more you try to deflect, the guiltier you look."

Daniel opened his mouth to repudiate this, but then snapped it shut again. I could see he was quickly thinking things through. He slowly said, "Okay. Look, the thing is, Bianca and I did have a pretty volatile relationship. It's true. But let's face it—we're both really passionate people who cared a lot about what we did for a living. We did have civil conversations with each other, but that's obviously not what people want to gossip about. Our relationship was over ages ago—it's ancient history. And if I didn't want to talk about how Bianca and I argued, well, that's human nature, isn't it? I'd rather focus on the good times we had together now that she's gone."

He put his arm around Holly again and seemed to notice for the first time that she was trembling. "Right now, I'm going to take Holly back home. She's had a terrible shock. I'm going to take care of her. You know where to find her if you need to ask her any questions about today."

Daniel steered Holly toward the parking lot. She stopped and tossed her keys to me so that Grayson and I could get back home later. Morrow watched them go.

Chapter Thirteen

Morrow turned to us. "Can you give me some background about your day today? What were you doing here? What were you doing before you came over?"

Grayson and I shared an uncomfortable look. Here I was again, right where and when another body was discovered. Outsider or not, I couldn't help but appear suspicious, I was sure.

"We were here at the beach, actually." I cleared my throat. "We'd heard about the Tuesday turtle walks and decided to join up."

Morrow quirked an eyebrow. "And Sierra Barnett was on the walk?"

"Yes, she was leading it along with a ranger," said Grayson.

Morrow considered us both for a few moments. "You were both at the community forum on the sand replenishment. Now, today, you were at the turtle talk with Sierra Barnett. You're not trying to investigate this case, are you? Play detective?"

"Not at all," Grayson and I chorused together.

Morrow seemed dubious. "You remember I warned you from doing that last time. Make sure you don't keep poking around. We're clearly dealing with a dangerous individual. I don't want to discover that either one of you has been murdered because you were asking too many questions. Let the police do our jobs."

We nodded.

"So, for whatever reason, you were on the turtle walk this morning. How did Sierra seem?" asked Morrow.

"Well, we didn't know her, obviously. But my friend Holly was acquainted with her and told us about the walks. As far as we know, Sierra seemed perfectly normal. She answered questions during the walk." I said.

"Did you speak with her on her own? Aside from during the official walk?" asked the detective.

Grayson said, "We did, after the walk had wrapped up. We introduced ourselves as friends of Holly's. She told us about how passionate she was about saving the turtles."

Morrow's expression seemed to say that he'd heard entirely too much on that particular subject. "Anything else? Anything regarding the case?"

Grayson glanced at me. "Sierra seemed sort of distracted to me when we were talking to her. Maybe like she had something on her mind. But like Ann said, we didn't know her."

Morrow said, "Okay. But aside from her demeanor, did she say anything about the investigation? Or Bianca's death?"

I didn't really want to throw Daniel under the bus, although Sierra had definitely said a few choice words about him. I figured if she'd told us about her suspicions about Daniel, she'd probably told the cops, too. After all, she'd have wanted to direct police interest away from herself. But I mentioned Sierra had talked a little about Nolan and how, in Sierra's opinion, Bianca had looked down on him as an archaeologist.

Morrow jotted down a couple more notes. "And you left the beach and returned?"

"That's right," said Grayson. "Sierra was planning on taking a walk on the beach. We headed back to Holly's house. But when we walked in, Holly was interested in going to the beach."

Morrow raised his eyebrow again. "So you decided to go back to the beach, even though you'd just left?"

We nodded.

"That seems like an odd choice," said Morrow. "May I ask why?"

I said slowly, "Holly had heard that a silver car had been outside Bianca Donovan's house the morning she'd been murdered. Holly knew the type of car Sierra drove because she was a client of hers from time to time."

Morrow's lips tightened. "How did she hear this?"

"She was out running errands and spoke with one of Bianca's neighbors who was doing yardwork. The neighbor told her that."

I wished I could see Morrow's eyes, but they were completely concealed behind the dark sunglasses. His voice was stern when he spoke, though. "So you decided to come back to the beach so your friend could question Sierra. Is that correct?"

"It's true, then?" asked Grayson, his journalistic tendencies coming forward. "Was Sierra Barnett there Saturday morning?"

Morrow said tersely, "It's true. The neighbor gave us the same information. I'm going to ask you to keep it under your hat, though. I don't want to see it on the six o'clock news, understand?"

We hastily agreed with him. I asked, "So are you thinking Sierra was at Bianca's house shortly before her murder? That she saw someone doing something incriminating?"

"I'm not going to speculate," said Morrow in a brusque voice. "I'd like to hear more about your friend Holly's morning."

I got very still. "Well, she was at the house when we left. Then she left to run errands. I'm sure Bianca's neighbor can vouch for the fact that she was speaking with her, too. Besides, she had no idea Sierra was dead. That's why Holly was heading back to the beach with us—to speak with Sierra."

Morrow made more notes in his notebook. I continued, feeling a little desperate, "Look, Holly didn't have any reason to kill Sierra. She was just an acquaintance of hers. Holly used her for the occasional massage."

Morrow' eyebrow sprang up once again. "It seems to me that you very effectively explained why *anyone* might want to kill Sierra. Sierra was at Bianca's house and might have identified the murderer. Besides, Holly had plenty of reasons to want Bianca Donovan gone. From everything I've heard, your friend's fiancé was still very much in contact with Bianca. Perhaps they were still seeing each other romantically."

"But we're Holly's alibi for Bianca's death," said Grayson in a reasonable voice.

Morrow shook his head. "Not all the time. Holly was awake first, from your account of that morning. While you were getting ready for the day or making those pancakes, she could easily have slipped away and murdered Dr. Donovan."

I said stoutly, "You're going to waste your time if you try following that line of inquiry. I can vouch for Holly's character. I've known her for years. There's absolutely no way she would kill anybody."

Morrow didn't seem impressed by my character reference. He was being called away by another officer when I said, "Wait a second. We took some pictures before the tide could wash away any potential evidence. I can send you the photos."

Morrow did want them, so I emailed them to his work email address. Then he walked off to join his colleague.

Grayson and I gave each other grim looks. Things were taking a turn for the worst. I was trying to help poke around a little, mainly for Holly, who was concerned about her fiancé being a suspect. But now it looked like Holly was considered a potential suspect, too.

A woman with bright red hair, a ruddy complexion, and a turtle team tee-shirt walked up to us. She was slightly out of breath from her quick walk down the beach. "I saw you talking with the cops," she said, an anxious tone in her voice. "Do you know what happened there? On the beach?"

"I'm afraid so," I said slowly. "I'm afraid someone drowned."

"Do you know who it was?" the woman's eyes were focused on us.

"It was Sierra Barnett. I'm sorry. It looks like you were on the turtle team together?" I asked.

The woman burst into tears as Grayson and I looked helplessly on. I didn't even have a tissue to offer her. I patted her gently on the back, and she reached out to enclose me in a bear hug as she cried for several minutes.

She managed to stop, using the back of her hand to swipe some tears from her face. "I'm so sorry. I was friends with Sierra. This is a terrible blow." She paused. "Was she out swimming?"

I shook my head. "I'm sorry," I said again. "It looks like it might have been foul play."

The woman's face was shocked. "Oh no. Oh, how awful."

We were quiet for a few moments, watching the police taking pictures and quickly working to collect as much information as possible as the tide kept relentlessly coming in.

The woman said in an absent voice, "I've been so worried about Sierra. Ever since that woman died."

"Bianca Donovan?" Grayson asked quietly.

"That's right. Sierra's been acting like a different person since Saturday. Jumpy, agitated, tearful. Almost guilty. Just nothing like herself at all. I could tell she had something on her mind. I was kind of confused about it." The woman paused. "Not to be impolite, but I thought Sierra might at least be relieved that the biggest opponent to the sand replenishment was removed. No one else cared nearly as much about the Stone Fleet as Bianca did."

I said, "Did Sierra talk at all about what was on her mind?"

The woman shook her head. "I wish she had. If she'd confided in me, maybe this wouldn't have happened. I should have pressed her more—should have asked more questions." She paused. "Sierra did say that she'd 'screwed up.'"

"What did you think she meant by that?" Grayson asked.

"I wasn't sure. She'd been so distracted. Last Sunday, she'd missed a turtle nest when she went out on patrol. It ended up being okay, but that was totally unlike Sierra." The woman looked at us. "Maybe that's what she meant when she said she'd screwed up? I wasn't sure what to say, you know? I kept hoping that, as time went on, that Sierra would get better. I figured maybe she just felt guilty about Bianca's death."

Grayson and I must have looked startled because the woman quickly said, "Not because she killed her, you understand. But because she'd had words with Bianca on quite a few occasions. For the sake of the turtles, you know."

I said, "I understood Bianca was also a client of Sierra's. For massages."

The woman nodded. "That's something else that worried me. Sierra always said Bianca was one of her best clients. I guess she must have had a lot of stress because Sierra would be working on her muscles at least once a week. Sierra owned her own business, and I didn't think she could afford to be running off good customers."

Grayson asked, "Sierra was bringing up the beach renourishment while she was giving Bianca massages?"

The woman made a face. "She said she didn't, but knowing Sierra, I couldn't imagine her being able to avoid the topic. Especially with Bianca being a captive audience. Like I said, Sierra cared a lot about the environment and the turtles." She started tearing up again. "I'd better go. I need to let the other members of the turtle team know."

After she walked off, Grayson and I walked back to Holly's car. "Want to drive?" he asked.

"Not especially," I admitted. "I feel like my head is about to explode."

"Too much information at once?"

I said, "Well, that too. But really, the problem is more that I've got a massive headache."

Unfortunately, I knew these kinds of headaches were demanding, not letting up until I'd retreated to a dark room somewhere. Usually I had to keep my eyes closed—I couldn't even read a book. So when we got back to Holly's house, I headed upstairs to take a couple of aspirin, close the blinds on the beautiful day, and try to take a nap. Fitz curled up next to my legs in sweet solidarity. Holly and Daniel were still out; presumably, Daniel had taken Holly to get a meal. Grayson took Murphy out for a walk.

It was over an hour later when I heard voices downstairs. I was relieved my headache had disappeared. I washed my face in the bathroom to wake up better, then I headed downstairs.

Holly was talking to Grayson as Murphy danced excitedly around at Holly's return. Holly gave me a smile when I joined them. "Headache better?" she asked sympathetically.

"All gone now," I said. "How are you holding up?"

Holly shrugged, but looked tense. "It's just been a really weird day. My mom and dad just got into town, too, and they want to take us out for lunch, if you and Grayson are up to it."

Grayson said, "That's nice of them. I think I'll stay back at the house, though, if that's okay. I know Ann would like the chance to catch up with your folks. I'll hang out here with Murphy and Fitz. Maybe watch a little TV."

Holly's parents came by to pick us up thirty minutes later. I'd changed clothes in the meantime and freshened up. Holly's folks always went out to amazing restaurants, and I didn't want to look like something the cat dragged in. They were great people. When I'd been at college with Holly, they'd come into town and take us out to eat, stepping in sometimes as surrogate parents, knowing I was living with my great aunt. And they always seemed very invested in me and my life.

They both gave me a warm hug when they saw me. "I'm so glad you're here," murmured Celeste, giving me a meaningful look. I had the feeling that I might hear more from her later.

They took us to a gorgeous restaurant in a meticulously restored historic building. We walked in under the soft glow of crystal chandeliers suspended from the high ceilings. There were polished marble floors, plush velvet banquettes, and intricately carved wood paneling. Lush flower arrangements were everywhere.

The server pulled out our chairs and filled our water glasses. Holly's dad, Maximillian, ordered bottles of wine for the table, which came out quickly.

Celeste took a sip of white wine, then said, "Holly, tell us more about what happened this morning."

This prompted Holly to burst immediately into tears. Her mother leaned over to draw her close to her while her father looked agitated. Max said, "Does this have anything to do with Daniel?"

This made Holly cry harder. The Walshes looked over at me to see if I could offer either information or help staunching the flood of tears. I cleared my throat. "Not directly, no. Right, Holly?"

Holly excused herself. "Sorry, I'll wash my face," she mumbled as she hurried away.

Chapter Fourteen

N ow the Walshes were both looking at me, worry etched across their faces. I took in a deep breath. I didn't want to say anything that Holly wouldn't want me to say, but I knew Celeste and Max wanted answers.

"Is she all right?" asked Celeste in an undertone. "I've never seen Holly in such a state."

I said, "I think she's doing okay. Not great, of course. But she's under a lot of stress."

"Stress?" Max's forehead furrowed. "What kind of stress? This is all about Daniel, isn't it?"

"I think it's a combination of things," I said honestly. "I'm guessing Holly mentioned the suspicious death at the beach this morning?"

"Yes, but she didn't say much. Only that she'd arrived on the beach at the same time as this incident. Is that part of what's making her upset?" asked Max. He looked as if he wanted to swoop in and fix all of Holly's problems, whatever they might be.

I glanced over toward the restroom, hoping Holly would suddenly reappear and tell her parents everything they wanted to hear. But there was no sign of her. I said slowly, "That's part of it, yes. Holly was acquainted with the woman who died. We'd gone to the beach so Holly could speak with Sierra about something. It was a shock to find that she'd died."

Celeste made a sympathetic noise. "Of course it was. How awful for Holly. And for you."

Max was still focused on finding exactly what might need fixing. "But am I right that, ultimately, this is all connected to Daniel?"

I hesitated, then nodded, unable to withstand Max's piercing blue stare. "Only tangentially, though. Did Holly mention there'd been a previous death?"

"We read about it in the newspaper. We still subscribe to the Post and Courier to keep up with local news. You're saying that Daniel was involved in *that* death? Of the state archaeologist?" Max's bushy eyebrows were high on his head.

"Not necessarily *involved*," I said quickly. "But he used to be in a relationship with Bianca Donovan."

Celeste and her husband gave each other knowing looks. "We knew he was no good," said Celeste softly.

I found myself in the strange position of having to defend Daniel. "Like I said, he's probably not involved at all. Naturally, the police have to consider all the angles. Because he was seeing Bianca previous to his relationship with Holly, the police would want to investigate that connection." I paused. "The important thing is that Holly's happy."

"*Is* she happy?" asked Max sharply. "You know we trust your opinion, Ann. If Holly's genuinely happy, then I'll back off and bless their union."

I hesitated. "She seems very happy when she's around Daniel." Most of the time.

Celeste seemed to be searching for something positive to say about her future son-in-law. "He's always been such a gentleman around me. Always bringing me flowers when I'm in town. Opening doors, waiting on me hand and foot."

Max grunted, clearly not impressed.

"I hope he's that way with Holly, too," said Celeste, looking across the table at me.

"He was this morning," I said truthfully. "Daniel was wonderful after we'd discovered Sierra was gone. He whisked her away and seemed determined to look after her."

Celeste looked down at her wineglass. "I just want everything to be okay. I want Holly to have a long, happy, healthy life." She gave Max a helpless look. "Holly's our only child now."

Max reached over to hold her hand. "We'll make sure it's okay. It's natural that we're investing all our worry in Holly now. But we know she can take care of herself. Besides, we have Ann here to keep an eye on Holly while this investigation is going on."

There was something unspoken in his words. I knew Max well enough to realize he was tasking me with not only looking after Holly, but keeping him in the loop, too. I didn't want to be a tattle-tale if things started going downhill for Holly and Daniel. On the other hand, though, we were all mutually invested in Holly's happiness.

Holly came back from the restroom, face scrubbed and looking better. She gave us an apologetic smile. "Sorry. I guess

I must not have gotten enough sleep last night. I'm usually not that emotional."

"Maybe you can turn in early tonight," said Celeste, looking at her daughter with concern.

"Actually, we're going to a thing tonight," said Holly. Then she gave me an apologetic look. "At least, I am. You and Grayson are invited, but I totally understand if you'd rather have a quiet night."

"We're probably up for it," I said. "What is it?"

"It's another gallery show. Daniel isn't featured in this one, but one of his friends is."

Max said, "So it was Daniel's idea to go out tonight?"

Holly looked a little defensive. "He thought it would be a good way to cheer me up after today."

Celeste apparently thought it was a nice time to change the subject. "Speaking of cheering you up, I thought it might be fun to go shopping after lunch. We could head to King Street or Charleston Place. What do you think?"

Holly's face brightened. "Do you think we could look for wedding dresses?"

I saw Max flinch, but fortunately, Holly missed it.

"Of course we can," said Celeste warmly.

Holly gave me an apologetic look again. "We could drop you off at the house first, Ann. You'll be bored to tears."

Holly knew me well. Shopping was never my favorite activity. But wedding dress shopping for my best friend was a little different. I shook my head. "I'd love to go along with you."

Holly looked dubious, but smiled at me.

We had an amazing lunch. I ordered the shrimp and grits, which were amazing with cheddar grits, Tasso ham, fennel, peppers, and onions. I nursed my one glass of wine, fearing I'd fall asleep at the bridal shops if I had more. But somehow, all the wine at the table was completely consumed by the Walshes. Tricky family conversations could do that, I supposed.

Soon Celeste, Holly, and I were walking into Belle Élégance Bridal Boutique. It was housed in a historic Charleston building with large bay windows on the front. The walls were in pastel hues, accented with delicate floral wallpaper and intricate crown molding. Antique mannequins showcased various dresses that all seemed to be masterpieces of lace, silk, and tulle.

A graceful, impeccably dressed woman named Isabella joined us to help Holly navigate through the different dresses. She offered us wine and water, then listened as Holly explained her preferences in terms of fit and style. Isabella set off briskly to bring back options.

"We'll go to a bookstore after this," said Holly, giving me a grin.

"No, this is fun," I protested.

Celeste said, "Actually, a bookstore *would* be nice, I think. A good friend of ours has a birthday coming up. Finding a marvelous book for him would make the perfect gift."

Isabella brought out an impressive number of dresses, and we spent the next hour and a half watching Holly model them. But although she looked beautiful in several of the dresses, Holly wasn't completely satisfied. She was looking for a basic, but classic dress and the gowns she was being shown didn't seem to match the image in her mind.

"To the bookstore!" said Holly, as we left the shop, dress-less.

The headache from earlier was intruding again. But I couldn't turn down the chance to visit a bookstore, especially since Celeste wanted to buy a gift there.

"We're going to a used bookstore, aren't we?" asked Celeste. Holly was leading the way.

"Are we?" asked Holly. "I thought you were getting a gift."

"Yes, but I want it to be something unusual. Not a brand-new book. Even better if it's signed."

It sounded like a tall order to me, but used bookstore owners are the best at tracking down exactly what customers are looking for. Better, definitely, than poor Isabelle at the bridal shop.

We walked down the street and down a flight of stairs to the basement of a brick building. The place gave the impression of being a speakeasy for literature. The interior, once we reached it, was lined floor to ceiling with books. A rather rickety and well-used wheeled library ladder stood in front of one wall. The owner had added vintage pieces that lent character to the shop, like antique lamps, old typewriters, and literary quotes in small frames alongside the books on the shelves. Instrumental jazz played softly in the background. The aroma of fresh coffee and old books mingled in the air.

Despite the hidden feel of the shop, there were quite a few customers inside, some sitting in cozy reading nooks with coffee cups in hand. A young man with wire-rimmed glasses and brown hair flopping in his face seemed to be on the staff. He was chatting with an older man about the book *The Goldfinch* and waving his hands enthusiastically as he talked up the novel. He wore well-worn jeans with a button-down shirt.

"Looks like he works here," said Celeste.

"Actually, I think he might be the owner," said Holly, watching him. "I've been here a couple of times before."

After bringing *The Goldfinch* to his customer, the young man spotted us watching him and came over with an easy smile. "May I help you find anything?"

"Is this your shop?" asked Celeste curiously.

"It is, actually. I'm Ben Carter. It was my uncle's bookstore for decades, until he retired and I bought it from him."

"What a wonderful place," said Celeste, clearly impressed. "I love the atmosphere here." She turned to me. "Ann here is a librarian."

It was always interesting being introduced as a librarian. People who were readers often jumped in, asking me questions about my favorite books or books I could recommend to them. But others reached the conclusion my job was boring (it was anything but), or that *I* was dull or uptight. But Ben beamed right away.

"One of my favorite places to hang out. I bet you love your job."

I nodded, smiling back at him. That was something that few people really understood. I loved being around books and introducing people to stories I loved. I had the feeling Ben felt the same way.

Celeste said, "To answer your question, I'm looking for a gift for a dear friend of mine. It would be especially nice if the book were signed, but it's not totally a deal-breaker if it's not."

"Got it," said Ben. "What's your friend like?"

"Intellectually curious. A big reader. He's eclectic in his reading, too. And rather quirky."

Ben considered this for a moment. "Several books come to mind. I do have a signed copy of *Fear and Loathing in Las Vegas* by Hunter S. Thompson. I also have an autographed copy of Tom Wolfe's *The Electric Kool-Aid Acid Test*. Would you like to see them?"

Celeste looked pleased. "You're good. I'd love to see the books." She followed him off into the stacks of books.

"Nice guy," I said in a vague voice, already getting distracted by the sheer number of amazing books around me. Before I meandered off to explore, I glanced over to see Holly watching Ben go, a conflicted look on her face.

We spent about an hour there. Ben started up a shy conversation with Holly, mostly book-related. Holly was quite a reader herself, so it sounded like a friendly talk. Celeste left with the Wolfe book, I left with *The Unbearable Lightness of Being* by Milan Kundera, and Holly left with a faint smile. I couldn't help but hope that she might be reconsidering her engagement with Daniel. I reminded myself again that my role was simply to be supportive, whatever Holly did.

We got back to Holly's house. Grayson had fallen asleep on the sofa in front of some kind of science fiction show. He woke abruptly, smiling. "Sorry. I guess I must have drifted off." He looked at his watch. "You must have enjoyed your lunch."

Holly grinned at him. "We did, but you'll be glad to know you were spared going bridal dress shopping afterwards."

"Oh, I'd have been up for that, but I don't think my opinion would have been worth much," said Grayson with a chuckle. "How did it go? Did you find a dress?"

Holly made a face. "No, I didn't have any luck. Or maybe I'm just too picky. I have this image in my head of a particular style of dress and now I'm starting to wonder if they even make it." She shrugged. "It's not a big deal. We don't even have a date set for the wedding."

"What's the plan for the rest of the day?" asked Grayson.

Holly said, "Well, I was telling Ann that Daniel invited us out tonight to a friend's gallery opening. He thought it might be nice if we go to supper before, near the gallery. But if y'all aren't up to it, Daniel and I could just go. It's been a long day for all of us."

Grayson looked over at me, trying to gauge what I wanted to do. But I was probably not giving him any clues, since I was feeling conflicted about it myself. I'd already told Holly that we'd go with her, so I gave him a small nod.

"I think we're up for it," said Grayson. "Sounds like a plan."

"In the meantime, I do have actual work to do," said Holly with a sigh. "In fact, I've got a remote meeting in twenty minutes."

We got out of Holly's hair, heading upstairs. I filled in Grayson in a quiet voice, telling him about Holly's parents and their concerns about Daniel. Grayson listened attentively, nodding. "It stinks, doesn't it? I know you were coming down here ready to find that Daniel was this awesome guy."

"Yeah. I really wanted him to be. For Holly's sake. She's always felt more like a sister to me than just a friend, you know? I didn't really have any close friends in high school, then she and I were so close in college. I kind of thought Daniel would be almost like a brother-in-law."

Grayson was quiet for a few moments. "Holly must care a lot about him, considering she knows how her parents feel about him."

"Well, and considering some of his treatment of her, too. He can be kind of rude and dismissive sometimes." I sighed. I thought again about Ben, the bookshop owner. He was much more the kind of guy I'd pictured when I'd thought about who Holly's fiancé might be. Kind, intellectual, warm. I shrugged. "Maybe tonight will be better. Daniel did seem really concerned about Holly this morning, when he took her away from the beach."

Grayson said dryly, "Maybe he wanted to get away from the beach because Morrow was questioning him."

"The thought had crossed my mind."

Grayson's eyes crinkled into a smile. "Isn't it great that we don't have these kinds of problems? Our relationship seems to really gel. At least, I think it does."

I smiled back at him. "It does." I gave him a hug. "Sorry you were on your own this afternoon."

"Oh, it was fine. I did run by my uncle's house again, just for a little while. I got a couple more things taken care of. Then I came back and just chilled out here."

I said wryly, "It's probably good you did. It sounds like we might be out late again tonight. I'll feel like being a total hermit when we get back home to Whitby."

"I'd be honored to be a hermit with you," said Grayson chivalrously.

"I'm not sure if that's how it works."

"Then I'll be as close to you as your hermit lifestyle allows."

Chapter Fifteen

That evening, Grayson and I got dressed for the gallery show. Grayson wore a blue button-down shirt and khakis. After some indecision on my end, I finally chose a cream blouse, tailored black blazer, and slim-fit black pants.

We joined Holly downstairs when it was time to meet up with Daniel for dinner. Holly took a more fun approach to her clothes, picking a geometric-print midi dress with oversized earrings.

"We look great!" Holly proclaimed. "Let's take a selfie."

We did and afterward, we headed out. Holly was in much better spirits, making happy small talk and telling funny stories. Her good mood was infectious and soon we arrived at the restaurant, laughing as we walked inside.

It was a completely different place than where we'd gone to lunch with Holly's parents. It was a bistro with a lot of old-world charm. The brick exterior had intricate wrought-iron detailing. Lush greenery spilled out of window boxes. A quaint chalkboard sign listed the specials written in elegant calligraphy. The interior was a blend of rustic allure and understated elegance.

Daniel was already there, sitting at a table for four covered with butcher block paper. He stood up, giving Holly a quick kiss, then gave Grayson and me a lazy grin. "Greetings. I trust the rest of your day went better than the start?"

I saw a small shadow flit across Holly's features at the indirect mention of Sierra's murder this morning. I quickly said, "We've had a great day. Nice lunch with Holly's folks."

Daniel's mouth twisted at the mention of the Walshes. Holly noticed and busied herself with looking at the menu. Grayson and I took her cue and started reading it ourselves. It looked like a thoughtfully curated selection of French-inspired dishes with a modern twist. There was a champagne poached pear salad with crumbled goat cheese, candied walnuts, and a honey drizzle. There was also a ratatouille Napoleon with layers of thinly sliced zucchini, eggplant, and roasted bell peppers stacked with goat cheese and roasted tomato coulis. I felt drawn to the vegetarian options for some reason.

"What's good here?" asked Grayson, smiling over at Daniel.

Daniel smirked. "Everything is good here. That's why I picked the place. But I especially like the duck confit tacos. They're topped with this nice, tangy citrus slaw."

The server came by and took our orders. Holly was telling Daniel about our afternoon. He was nodding, but his eyes were scanning the restaurant. He suddenly straightened up, interrupting Holly with, "Oh, Cooper's here."

He stood up to shake Cooper Thornton, the local developer's, hand. Cooper clapped him on the back, then greeted the rest of us. "How are all of you doing tonight?"

"We're great," said Daniel. "We're heading to James Reynolds' show after dinner."

Cooper nodded. "That's at the Loft Gallery, isn't it? Abstract paintings and whatnot?"

Daniel said, "That's right. You'd love it. James is all about bold colors and dynamic compositions. He wants to connect with viewers on a visceral level. He has interactive installations, too. You're going, right?"

"Can't do it this time, buddy. Elana and I are meeting up after this with some business friends for drinks." He gestured to a younger, elegantly dressed woman with mischievous eyes and wearing an emerald-green cocktail dress with strappy sandals who was laughing at something a friend at another table was saying. "Drink a glass of champagne for me." Cooper made a face. "I probably need it. "This week has been off to a rotten start."

Cooper seemed to want to say more. Even Daniel, who wasn't particularly intuitive with anyone else, appeared to realize this. "Sierra Barnett's death today. Awful. You were acquainted, weren't you?"

"No, no. Of course, we were on the same side of the sand replenishment issue. I knew who she was and that she was very vocal with the turtle group. I might have briefly spoken to her at a town hall meeting once." Cooper frowned in thought, then nodded. "That's right. A government meeting of some kind. I donated money to the turtle team after hearing her speak at a public forum."

Daniel gave a short laugh. "Are the cops harassing you like they're harassing me?"

Cooper rolled his eyes. He said in a jocular voice, "I wish the cops would give me a heads-up whenever I need to have an alibi. I just can't keep up. I'm terrible with having them. I was asleep this morning when Sierra died. I'd been up late last night dancing at a club. Elana really likes dancing."

At that point, Elana came over to join us. She introduced herself to Grayson and me, nodded at Holly, and gave Daniel a hug. Holly's eyes were chilly as she watched the two of them chat and laugh together. Cooper, on the other hand, didn't seem concerned about Elana and Daniel. Maybe he felt confident enough in his wealth and power.

There was a bit of an awkward silence between Grayson, Cooper, and I while Daniel and Elana chatted. Finally, Grayson, always game to make situations easier, said, "Do you two go dancing often?"

"All the time!" said Cooper with a grin. "I'm thinking I'm going to end up losing weight in the process. We were out forever. I just couldn't keep up."

It wasn't too surprising, I thought uncharitably. Cooper should probably date someone his own age if he wanted to keep up with them.

Daniel and Elana finally rejoined the conversation. "Sorry," said Daniel. "We were talking about the beach replenishment, weren't we?"

"Sort of. Anyway, you know how important it is to the local economy. You know everybody in town, Daniel, so talk it up when you can. It's not just to help out the property values for the residents and businesses along the coastline. It creates a major tourism boost for the entire area. Tourists want to know there's plenty of beach to jog on or to sunbathe on. It also helps the environment, you know? It prevents erosion, mitigates storm damage, and preserves dunes and marshes. Plus, you have to realize the job creation, even on a temporary level, that beach renourishment provides."

It sounded a little like Cooper was giving a speech, and one he'd given many times before. Elana must have thought the same thing, because she was hiding a yawn behind her hand.

"Bianca might have disagreed, but I've always considered myself something of a history buff," continued Cooper. "World War II is my particular interest. Bianca always thought I didn't care anything about preserving the Stone Fleet. She couldn't have been more wrong. I felt it needed an exhibit in a local museum. Or at least a plaque." His eyebrows drew together as he considered this. "Maybe my foundation can give something like that in memory of Bianca." Then he looked even more thoughtful. "You know, it would also be nice to set up donations for the turtle team in Sierra's memory. That way, it's fair on both sides of the issue."

Daniel said, "Sounds like a good idea. So you're thinking the beach replenishment is going to go through now that Bianca isn't standing up for preservation?"

Cooper shrugged. "Why not? She was the chief opponent against the renourishment. Nolan Harper, who's elected himself spokesperson for the Stone Fleet, isn't nearly as knowledgeable or as dedicated. I foresee the project moving ahead soon." He gave Daniel a thoughtful look. "Any thoughts on what might have happened to Bianca?"

Elana gave a surprised laugh. "Cooper! You're making it sound like Daniel murdered that woman."

Cooper laughed with her, showing off rows of perfect white teeth. "Yeah, that didn't come out right. Even though Daniel was always scrapping with Bianca over something. I meant to ask if you had ideas on other suspects. Maybe you and I can figure out a way to get the cops off our tails."

Daniel gave a short laugh, not as amused as Cooper seemed to be. "Well, I guess maybe that Eleanor woman. She was never Bianca's biggest fan."

Cooper wagged a finger at him. "That's exactly what I told the police. Like I mentioned before, Eleanor Johnson was real big on that development project. She spoke to me right after Bianca's death, wanting to see if we could move things forward."

I cleared my throat. "Eleanor believes the development can go ahead now? That there won't be any other issues with historic preservation?"

Cooper said, "She does. I don't know if she's being optimistic, though. Bianca was definitely the one who was spearheading the preservation efforts on the Johnson property. She had her finger in a lot of pies. Anyway, Eleanor has been blowing up my phone lately. She wants to make money, of course, but because she'll be right next door to the development, she also wants to make sure it's a nice subdivision."

Elana's eyes were bright. "Maybe she had something to do with Bianca's death. I watch a lot of detective and cop shows on TV. It's really cool to be this close to a case."

Cooper frowned. He clearly didn't enjoy being the reason that Elana was close to a murder inquiry. Nor that she seemed so entertained by it.

"Did I tell you when we were out for lunch, people kept giving you suspicious looks?" Elana asked Cooper cheerfully.

"I'm sure you were imagining it," said Cooper coolly.

"I figured it was probably because you and Bianca used to date."

Now Cooper turned a full, icy glare on the young woman. "That wasn't public knowledge and didn't last long."

But Elana didn't seem rebuffed at all. She waved and smiled to someone across the restaurant who she knew.

Before we left for the gallery, I ducked into the restroom. Elana was in there, reapplying makeup. She turned to me with a smile that seemed slightly tipsy. "Oh, hi there."

"Hi again," I said with a smile. "Hope you two have a nice evening."

Elana made a face. "Probably not. Cooper is 'conducting business.' As usual."

"No dancing tonight?" I asked lightly. "I understand Cooper was out late dancing with you last night."

Elana gave a scoffing laugh. "As if. He always tries to get mileage out of saying that. I can tell you he definitely wasn't dancing the night away with me. Cooper worked the room, as usual, then he left early. I ended up dancing with other people while he went home and went to sleep."

"So he didn't sleep in this morning?" The morning of Sierra's death.

"Cooper? Sleep in? That guy is programmed to get up at five o'clock every morning." Elana carefully reapplied her mascara.

"Well, hope your night tonight goes okay, at any rate." I smiled at her and slipped out. It seemed like no one had a good alibi for Sierra's death.

Chapter Sixteen

A little over an hour later, we'd finished eating our admittedly delicious food. Cooper had steered Elana over to their table when our food arrived. The gallery show was called "Reflections in Color: A Journey Through Emotion," and it was aptly named. The art fairly leaped from the canvas. A lot of the paintings almost seemed to move when you looked at them.

James Reynolds, the artist friend of Daniel's, gave a heartfelt and modest speech, thanking everyone for coming. And, although we were stuffed from our meal at the bistro, the food tempted us to eat a little more. There were smoked salmon canapés, caprese skewers, and miniature crostini.

The only problem with the evening was Daniel. After speaking with James, he'd been immediately accosted by a young woman in a flowing bohemian chic dress. Her delicate tattoos of various symbols peeked out from her sleeves. Wisps of loose, tousled hair framed her effortlessly beautiful face. Daniel seemed absolutely enchanted, reaching out frequently to touch her arm or laugh.

Holly's own face fell. She turned away. "I'm going to get a glass of champagne," she said in a falsely cheerful voice. "Anybody want one?"

Grayson and I shook our heads. Grayson said to me in a low voice, "I'm about to have a chat with that guy."

"Unfortunately, it's not like it would change who he is. If you talk to him, he might just behave a little better tonight. Or maybe not." I shrugged. "I'm hoping Daniel is just presenting enough evidence against himself that Holly realizes she might be making a mistake."

Holly came back with her glass of champagne. Her eyes were suspiciously bright.

Grayson said to her, "Want to drink that down and then head out? We've seen the exhibit, after all. I'll drive us all back."

Holly looked grateful. "Would you? I'll just slam this drink and we'll get back home. I suddenly want to see Murphy. That's the thing about dogs. They're always excited to see you." She downed her drink.

Daniel finally tore his gaze away from the young woman he was speaking to. He lifted a finger to her, asking her to wait, then hurried in our direction. "You're leaving?" he asked in a disbelieving voice. "We practically just got here."

Holly said, "I've seen everything I want to see."

Daniel looked uncertain, as if wondering if that was some sort of dig. "There's another show later this week."

Irritation flashed in Holly's eyes. "The problem is that I find out about everything last-minute." It sounded to me like she was redirecting her anger onto a smaller issue to avoid challenging Daniel on his flirting.

"The shows are all listed online."

"Maybe," said Holly, "but that doesn't mean I know which ones you're interested in going to. Which artists are your friends. Because I have no idea. Then I have to decide that day."

Daniel shrugged. "We could sync our calendars, I guess. I always have everything I want to see on my online calendar."

"Okay, fine. That would work better than what we're currently doing."

Daniel glanced back toward the young woman, who seemed to wait to finish their conversation. "Do you have something to write with?" he said impatiently.

I dug around in my purse, pulled out a small notebook and a pen, and handed them to Holly. Holly jotted down the password for Daniel's calendar.

"I'll look out for an invitation to synch them," he said distractedly. And with that, he was gone, heading back to continue his chat.

Holly seemed to square her shoulders as we walked to the car. Grayson took us back as I made a determined and desultory conversation on the way, which Holly responded to with absent murmurs. Then she got on her phone, looking at the piece of paper she was holding with Daniel's password on it.

Daniel apparently was in-between conversations with attractive women because Holly's phone dinged nearly immediately with a confirmation for the calendar synch. For the rest of the car ride, Holly was deep in Daniel's calendar.

Then she turned to me, her face white. "He's been lying to me."

Chapter Seventeen

"What do you mean?" I asked. Grayson pulled slowly into Holly's driveway.

Holly waved her phone. "He has all these sessions with Sierra loaded into his calendar. He *knew* her." She opened the car door, slamming it with more force than was necessary.

Grayson and I hurried in behind her. Murphy bounded up, putting his paws on Holly's shoulders and licking her face. She laughed and cried at the same time, tears trickling down her cheeks. Fitz watched the scene with concern from across the room, his green eyes narrowed.

Holly asked Grayson, "Do you mind grabbing that bottle of wine in the fridge? I believe I'm going to need it. And if y'all drink some too, that will keep me from consuming the whole thing."

Grayson came back in a minute with several glasses of white wine and the remainder of the bottle. I foraged around for a box of tissues and, finding it, thrust it at Holly. She took one and swabbed her face with it.

"Okay," Holly said, taking a deep breath. "I just need to settle down."

"Take your time," I said.

Holly did, taking a couple of sips of wine and composing herself. Murphy threw himself enthusiastically in her lap, snuggling his head against her shoulder.

"Okay," Holly said again. "So, Daniel knew Sierra."

"Was it just professionally?" asked Grayson. "You said 'sessions.' Does that mean he was seeing Sierra for massages?"

Holly shrugged, looking weary. "Sure, that could be it. It could be something completely innocent. But the problem is that he should have mentioned it. He knew I used Sierra for massages. If that's all it was, a business relationship, then it seems like he'd have mentioned it in some kind of offhand way. It seems more likely that they were having an affair. And that's not the only problem." She looked over at me.

"Daniel said he didn't know Sierra," I said slowly.

Holly threw up her hands. "Here I was trying to keep Daniel from being a suspect, and it sounds like he's actually a *great* suspect. Maybe Sierra was threatening to expose their relationship to me. Maybe he felt like he needed to shut her up."

"Now we're just speculating," I said. I felt the need to put on the brakes, even though I didn't think Daniel was good enough for Holly.

Grayson offered, "Maybe Daniel was trying to set up a massage as a gift for you? Maybe those were just reminders on his calendar to get in touch."

Holly gave him a small smile. "Thanks for trying to make me feel better. I can tell by the appointments that that's not what was going on, though." She threw her hands in the air. "Am I engaged to a murderer?"

We were all quiet for a few moments. Then Grayson said, "How about if I let you two talk it out a little? Maybe you can make sense of it all." He took his glass of wine, gave me a smile, and headed upstairs.

Murphy was still looking at Holly with soulful dog eyes, aware she was feeling a lot of different, uncomfortable emotions. He nuzzled his furry face against her neck.

Holly gave a short laugh. "Here you are in Charleston to celebrate my engagement, and I'm about to either have a fiancé in prison or a broken engagement. Or both." She looked at me with exhausted eyes. "I've been so dumb, Ann. I've been feeling like something is wrong with our relationship for the last few weeks. Right after we got engaged. But I've been burying that sense of intuition. All I've wanted to do is to just feel happy. I haven't *been* happy, though. That's the problem."

"You haven't been dumb," I said. "You've just been in love."

Holly sighed. "I think part of it is that I've been so busy with work and getting ahead that I haven't really had many meaningful relationships. So when one cropped up, I went totally overboard with it, hook, line, and sinker. Now it's easy for me to see that Daniel is a liar and a terminal flirt, if not a terminal cheater."

"What are you going to do?" I asked.

Holly thought it over for a few quiet moments. "I don't know. I really want to be in a relationship. I got pretty lonely with work being my main social outlet. But it's not worth being in a relationship when it's this stressful. Right now, I feel like I can't be sure where Daniel is and what he's up to. Obviously, I need to have a serious talk with him. But I'm feeling like I need to bring our engagement to an end." She gave another dry laugh.

"At least we haven't had any engagement parties or anything. That would make ending our engagement even more embarrassing."

"Everybody would understand, regardless," I said firmly. "Your friends just want you to be happy."

Holly nodded. "I'm so glad you're here. Thanks for helping me figure all this out."

"That's what friends are for," I said. I made a face. "Okay, that's really trite, but it's trite because it's true."

Murphy licked Holly's face in agreement and we both laughed.

Chapter Eighteen

The next morning, nobody rose early after all the emotion of the night before. Fitz purred in my ear after nine a.m., reminding me gently that his tummy was empty and that he'd really appreciate having it refilled. I tiptoed downstairs, Fitz bounding after me. After letting Murphy out to potty, I fed both of them, taking a stab at how much to feed the golden retriever. He seemed delighted with what was in his bowl, giving me a worshipful look, so it was possible I might have overdone it.

I opened a window in the kitchen, and Fitz happily perched on the sill, watching people walking their dogs down the street and driving off to work. I made a pot of coffee, followed by cheesy eggs and bacon with a side of grits. The smell of the bacon must have wafted upstairs because soon Holly and Grayson were downstairs.

"Good morning," I said cheerfully. "Help yourselves. I've made more food than we probably need."

Holly headed right for the coffeepot. "Oh, I doubt you've made too much food. I'm totally ravenous this morning. Probably something to do with my life falling completely apart yesterday." She looked at both of us with a wry smile. "Don't worry.

I feel a lot better this morning. I'm more in 'tackle the problem' mode. Excuse me if I seem distracted. I'm figuring out exactly how I'm going to approach Daniel later today."

"Can you take the day off from work?" I asked. I knew Holly had a pretty flexible schedule, but I couldn't see how she was going to focus on working with her relationship with Daniel spinning through her mind all the time.

"Unfortunately, not." Holly made a face as she heaped eggs and grits on her plate. "It's supposed to be no-meeting-Wednesday, but somehow everybody at work has forgotten about that. I looked on my online agenda and my morning and early afternoon are booked. I've already missed one meeting by oversleeping." She shrugged. "Fortunately, it wasn't anything important. Not something I was supposed to speak during, anyway." She snapped her fingers. "Oh, I wanted to tell y'all that Bianca Donovan's memorial service is going to be this morning. Eleven o'clock, I think. I saw it on my social media."

I said, "Got it. I know I didn't actually meet Bianca, but I feel like I might want to go, considering I found her. It might be nice to find some closure there."

Grayson said, "I'll go with you, Ann."

Holly pulled out her phone. "I bet I can take my lunch break then and go, too. But I'll need to drive in a separate car so I can get back home for my one o'clock meeting. I didn't really know Bianca, but I know Vicky, Bianca's sister. I know she and Bianca were really close. It would be good if I could make it."

Holly looked at the clock, groaned, and headed off to log into her meeting, plate of food in hand. Grayson and I took a more leisurely approach, sipping our coffee, petting the animals, and eating our fill. We took a walk around the neighborhood with Murphy in tow. The dog grinned the whole way. It wasn't exactly exercise, at least for Grayson and me, because Murphy was stopping to sniff about every five feet. But it was a gorgeous morning, and we were in no hurry.

"Holly seems better this morning," said Grayson.

"For sure. I guess sleeping on it helped. And everything looks a little brighter in the morning, too." I looked over at him. "You sure you want to go to the memorial service? You don't have to."

Grayson said, "It's no problem. I don't have anything else to do, and I'd like to spend my free time with you."

We lazed around Holly's place for a while before the memorial service. Then we got ready to head out in separate cars, as Holly had mentioned.

The service was packed. It was held at the historic St. Michaels' Episcopal Church. The Gothic architecture inside was impressive. The church was adorned with flickering candles and bouquets of white lilies. A string quartet played old hymns in the background. Holly whispered, "I recognize some people here. Looks like there are a good number of local government folks in attendance."

She'd been looking around since we'd arrived. I figured she wanted to see if Daniel had made the service. I didn't see him there, which was probably a good thing. I figured Holly probably wanted to plan exactly what she wanted to say to him. And a memorial service definitely wasn't the best venue for any kind of confrontation.

The service was well-thought through, despite Bianca's sudden and unexpected death. Bianca's favorite Bible verses were read by her parents and sister, emphasizing themes of perseverance, discovery, and the eternal nature of the human spirit. We sang "Amazing Grace" and "How Great Thou Art." Then there were personal reflections on Bianca's life from her close friends, family, and colleagues. They shared anecdotes from Bianca's childhood, memories of Bianca throughout the years, Bianca's contributions to archaeology, and her impact on their lives.

I saw Nolan Harper, the amateur archaeologist, sitting near the front of the sanctuary and wondered if he'd be one of the speakers. But he never rose to say anything.

There was a reception following at her sister's house, with her address listed on the program. "Will you be able to make it?" I asked. The service had taken a little over an hour, and I knew Holly had a meeting she'd mentioned.

Holly, frowning, checked her phone. Then she relaxed. "The one o'clock got canceled. I can stay at the reception for a little while, but then I need to make it back for the next meeting. I'll meet you over there."

Grayson and I followed Holly over. "I hope there's going to be enough parking," said Grayson, noticing the number of cars heading over to the reception.

"And enough room in the house. This is quite a crowd."

Grayson said, "Maybe they'll have tents in the yard."

Vicky Donovan's house and grounds put our worries to rest. There were two men with yellow vests directing traffic to a large field to the right of the house. The house itself was sizable, with a welcoming wrap-around porch holding rocking chairs and adorned with hanging flower baskets. We could see from our approach to the house that there was a winding garden pathway leading to the backyard where there were indeed tents, along with azalea bushes and magnolias.

We parked and joined Holly to walk to the back of the house. There, people were walking around solemnly with plates of ham biscuits, chicken and gravy, and fruit. Nolan Harper was standing by himself, looking rather awkward. He brightened when he spotted Grayson and me. I guess he must have realized we didn't know anyone either. Although it seemed like Nolan should certainly have known some of Bianca's former colleagues who were milling about.

"Good to see you," he said to us, as if he knew us well.

We introduced Holly to him, and Nolan shook her hand.

"A terrible business," said Nolan. "And now another death just yesterday." He shook his head. Then he looked curious. "Am I to understand that you were the ones who discovered Sierra Barnett?"

I said, "We were just close by when she was discovered."

"On the scene, then."

"That's right," I said.

"I couldn't believe it when I heard the news. Unbelievable." He tilted his head curiously at me. "I'm sure the police were interested in speaking with you. Considering you were also there when Bianca was found."

"They did want to ask me a few questions," I said wryly. "How about you? Did the police follow up with you?"

Nolan shrugged, but looked uncomfortable. "They did. I guess that's their standard procedure. At least, they made it sound as if it was."

Someone dropped a glass on the brick patio, making Nolan jump. He whirled around, relaxing when he saw it was just a broken glass. He certainly was jumpy for someone who had nothing to hide.

"Were you able to give the police an alibi?" Grayson asked in a friendly tone. "Ann and I couldn't, since we were out on the beach that morning."

Nolan shook his head. "No, I was at home still getting ready for my day."

"What's your day job?" asked Holly in a curious voice. "I guess your passion is probably archaeology. Do you do anything with it for your regular job?"

Nolan looked regretful. "No. I wish I did. I'm an accountant for my day job. A CPA. But I hang out with the archaeology organizations as often as I can. There are a lot of remote meetings, so that works out well." He sighed. "Of course, the remote meeting I was on around Bianca's death apparently didn't work out as an alibi, either. Apparently, it started after her murder. But I didn't know when the murder happened, after all."

"Have you been following the investigation closely?" I asked.

"Oh, no. I've been very busy, you know. Of course, I had no reason to harm Bianca Donovan. And I didn't even know Sierra, except by reputation. I hear she was very good at what she did. It has to be a very simple person who resolves differences through physical violence."

The three of us all murmured in agreement. Nolan continued, "Civil discourse, the sharing of ideas and even disagreements leads to personal growth, after all. I think Bianca and I
had a lot of mutual respect for each other."

That hadn't been what I understood, but I smiled and nodded with the others. Holly said sweetly, "That's a good thing. I
understood that you both had professional disagreements from
time-to-time."

Nolan flushed. "We did have some differences of opinion regarding archaeological methods. But we also enjoyed hearing an
opposing point of view."

Holly said, "Did you have any ideas about who might have
wanted to harm Bianca?"

Nolan snorted. "Well, originally, I'd thought it had to be
Sierra. She seemed like Bianca's most vocal opponent, after all.
But now it appears I'm wrong. There's somebody else who
wasn't crazy about Bianca. That guy she used to date."

We all froze. "Daniel?" croaked Holly.

"Right. That's the one. There's just something wrong about
that guy. He had a very contentious relationship with Bianca.
Turbulent is probably a better word."

Holly nodded silently. Nolan took that as encouragement
and continued. "I remember this one particular time. It was after
a meeting in front of city hall, when we were trying to get more
allocation for archeology projects. Daniel was present to argue
for arts funding. As per usual, the city gave in to the arts. I could
tell Bianca was furious, but she was holding it in really well.
Then Daniel came up and started taunting her about the funding."

"Taunting her," repeated Holly.

"That's right. He was throwing it in her face that he 'won.'" Nolan shook his head. "Totally immature. He was always like that around Bianca. And people think that *I* had a rocky relationship with Bianca?" He snorted again. "People will believe what they want to believe, though. That's why I made it a point to come to the service today. There were no hard feelings between me and Bianca."

Holly said, "Got it. Well, it was good talking to you. I should speak with Vicky before I head back home for a meeting. Take care."

As we walked over to speak with Bianca's sister, I could feel Nolan's gaze on us, watching.

Chapter Nineteen

Vicky was an attractive woman with dark hair and eyes. She seemed just slightly stunned, as if she had a tough time accepting that she was at her sister's memorial service. Almost as if she was politely going through the motions.

Holly gave her a hug and introduced Grayson and me. Vicky was giving us a courteous greeting when she paused. "Ann," she said thoughtfully. "Are you the one who found my sister?"

I nodded. "I'm so sorry. I've heard such great things about Bianca. What a terrible loss."

Vicky's eyes teared up. "Yes. We'd all been so proud of my sister. I'm not sure how my parents are ever going to recover from the blow. That's one reason I wanted to have the memorial service. I thought maybe it would offer them some closure."

She leaned over, looking at me. "Can you tell me how you found Bianca? The police didn't offer many details. All I've heard has been from the news reports, and they sound so gruesome and frightening."

I said, "It wasn't a gruesome and frightening scene at all. The only reason I felt something was wrong was because she and I had an appointment, and Bianca wasn't coming to the door.

Once I walked inside, there were no signs of a struggle. And when I saw your sister, I had to check for a pulse to make sure she hadn't simply fainted."

It was more information than I'd give to anyone else, knowing the police wanted to keep details quiet. But I knew I'd done the right thing when a look of relief crossed Vicky's features. "Thank you," she said simply. "I'll let my parents know, too. That will be a comfort to them."

Holly asked, "Vicky, have the police told you whether they have any leads?"

Vicky shook her head. "I haven't been in contact with them much. Of course, they told me when Sierra Barnett died. Awful. I hope they find out who did this soon. I don't think my parents and I can begin to move forward with our lives until they do."

Holly still had more questions. I had the feeling that now she was asking, not because she was trying to exonerate Daniel from culpability, but because she wanted to find out if she'd been engaged to a murderer. "Did Bianca talk at all about anyone bothering her in the days leading up to her death? Did the two of you talk frequently?"

"We did. We spoke the morning Bianca died, actually, since we were both early risers. That's how I remember your name, Ann. Bianca was looking forward to meeting with you and talking about the survey. We were on the phone with each other when Eleanor Johnson came by the house. Ringing the doorbell imperiously."

"You told the police this?" asked Holly.

"Of course. The cops told me that Eleanor said she left Bianca's house and returned later when she didn't get an answer.

Bianca had peeked out a window, seen Eleanor out there, and just picked back up with our conversation without answering the door. Bianca said the last way she wanted to start her day was by talking to Eleanor."

Our conversation was interrupted by an older woman with beautifully styled white hair. She patted Vicky on the back as if she were a labrador. "Oh goodness, I'm just so sorry about your dear sister. Such a terrible, terrible time."

"Thank you, Mrs. Williams." Vicky briefly introduced us, explaining that Mrs. Williams was Bianca's neighbor. She was not the one I'd spoken with, but apparently several houses down.

"I believe I heard you speaking about Eleanor Johnson when I was walking up," said the old woman innocently. But there was a sparkle in her eyes that indicated she was eager to hear any sort of gossip related to the case.

Vicky must have realized this, because she tried to minimize what Mrs. Williams had overheard. "Oh, that's nothing. Eleanor came up to the house before my sister died, but she left right after that."

"She did *not* leave right after that," said Mrs. Williams in her sweet little old lady voice. "Eleanor proceeded to leave her car right in front of my house. I do like to reserve the spaces in front of my house for my own visitors, you understand. I may not have many of them, but I want them to easily visit me. And Eleanor parked on my grass."

"I'm sorry to hear that," said Vicky. Although Vicky appeared to be trying to hide a smile.

Grayson and I looked at each other. If Eleanor never left, was she the one who murdered Bianca?

Someone else came up to speak with Vicky. We hastily offered our condolences, then stepped away.

Holly looked at her watch. "I think I'm going to grab some food to eat on the way home. That way I can hop into that meeting without feeling like I'm starving to death." She gave us a rueful look. "Sorry that I made you come in separate cars. I could have driven all of us."

Grayson said, "You didn't know your meeting was going to be canceled." He looked at me. "Want to grab anything?"

I shook my head. "I have some leftovers in the fridge that I should probably eat."

"We'll catch up with you back at the house, Holly," said Grayson.

"You've still got the key?"

"Right here."

Grayson and I headed back to Holly's house. Once there, we heated some leftover food and had some lunch. Holly didn't immediately make it back, which I thought was a little odd. I figured she'd just grab some ham biscuits and be a few minutes behind us.

Finally, she came in, looking distracted. "I've got to hop on that meeting, but I found out something. Lieutenant Morrow was talking to Nolan near the buffet. Apparently, Nolan and Sierra are neighbors. Like, right across the street from each other."

"What?" I asked. "He said he didn't know her."

"Well, apparently, that was a total lie. Morrow said there were emails on Sierra's phone to Nolan, talking about neighborhood stuff. Morrow was giving him a hard time about lying about their relationship." Then Holly rushed over to her computer to connect to her meeting.

Grayson said slowly, "So, are we thinking that Nolan killed Bianca and Sierra?"

I said, "I just don't know. Let's say he did go by Bianca's house and have an argument with her. Maybe he was sick of her belittling his interest in archeology. He got in there, lost control, and killed Bianca. Where does Sierra fit into the equation? We know she was there and then left."

Grayson said, "Maybe Sierra came by to give Bianca a massage. But Bianca didn't answer the door—because she was already dead."

I thought this through. "Then Sierra decides she must have gotten the date or time wrong. She's backing up out of the driveway and sees Nolan leaving Bianca's house. She doesn't think anything of it until she learns later that Bianca has been murdered. Then she realizes Nolan must have done it."

Grayson added, "And she knows who Nolan is because they're neighbors."

"Nolan has to murder her to make sure she doesn't tell the police what she knows," I continue.

"Or maybe Sierra tried blackmailing him," said Grayson.

"She might even have blackmailed him saying she wanted him to support the sand replenishment. Nolan isn't the state archaeologist, but he speaks at a lot of those meetings. It would have really made a statement if he'd supported the beach renourishment over the Stone Fleet."

My mind was whirling with possibilities. Grayson glanced over at me. "It's been a rough last few days. Holly's going back to deal with work. How about if we head over to the library and chill out for a while? That always makes you feel better."

I gave him a wry look. "It mostly feels better when I step behind the desk and start working."

"I'm sure they'd really appreciate some free labor." Grayson grinned at me.

"Sure, let's swing by there. I can read through the periodicals for a while. And there's always the South Carolina room. We can find out more about the Stone Fleet."

Grayson said, "Although that has nothing to do with our goal of relaxing and putting the case out of our heads for a little while."

Actually, removing the investigation from our minds apparently wasn't on the table at all. When we arrived at the library, I noticed a particular car.

"I think that's Eleanor Johnson's car," I said slowly. "No, I'm *sure* it's her car. She has a bumper sticker that says 'Palmetto State Pride' on it." I turned to him. "Let's talk with her before we start our chilling out project. I'd like to hear what she makes of Sierra Barnett's death."

Chapter Twenty

Grayson and I walked into the library. The smell of old books was already calming me down and centering me. "She's probably in the South Carolina room," I said. "It sounds like she spends a lot of time conducting research."

Sure enough, we found Eleanor upstairs. She was wearing a pastel floral dress, the family crest pendant, and her reading glasses. She frowned as we walked in, then recognition crossed her features.

"It's you," she said to me, removing her reading glasses. "The woman who found Bianca."

"Ann," I said, nodding. "And this is Grayson. It's good to see you again, Mrs. Johnson."

"Oh, call me Eleanor. I was just doing a little research on one of Charles's forebearers."

She clearly wanted to talk about the family history. Since my motive was to make her comfortable enough to talk about Sierra's death, I asked, "What kinds of things have you found out about the Johnson family? I'm sure you must have made all kinds of interesting discoveries over the years."

"Heavens, yes. The Johnson family forebearers fought for our nation's independence. They were Revolutionary War patriots. They were also one of the founding families here in Charleston." Eleanor described all the contributions various family members had made in Charleston culture, politics, and philanthropic endeavors.

Grayson was looking a bit drowsy. I moved on so he wouldn't start nodding off right in front of Eleanor. "That's really wonderful. It must be inspirational knowing that the family has weathered tough times and made it through, better and stronger than before."

Eleanor considered this. "Yes, I suppose it does. I hadn't thought of it that way. We're certainly going through a rather odd patch right now, what with Bianca's death." Her lips pursed.

I added, "And Sierra Barnett's."

"Yes, Sierra's, too."

I asked, "I know the police were probably following up with everyone they spoke to the first time around. Were you able to provide them with an alibi for Sierra's death?"

Eleanor looked at me askance. "I'm certain they had no suspicions whatsoever that I was involved with that. But no, I had a tough time getting out of the bed yesterday morning. Some days are like that. I'm on the go all day long, then sometimes I'll research until the wee hours of the morning. It means I'm not able to rise as early as I might like to." She raised her chin. "But like I mentioned, it's hardly an issue. After all, you saw me when I arrived at Bianca's house."

I said sternly, "I thought I did. But now I've heard from a witness that you never really left. Maybe you just took a stroll down the street and came back up."

Eleanor's eyes widened, and she looked panicked. "The witness doesn't know what she saw. That's the problem. Did she say she told the police?"

It was interesting that Eleanor assumed the witness was a woman. Perhaps she'd noticed her during her stroll. "She didn't say. Why *did* you go to Bianca's house then return?"

Eleanor slumped in her seat, looking exhausted. "Let me tell you what I saw. I did arrive at Bianca's house. I rang the doorbell, didn't get a reply, then decided to run an errand and return. I thought perhaps Bianca was still waking up or showering or something. When I returned from my errand, I saw a silver car in her driveway and knew I'd never get Bianca to the door to speak to me while she had company. So I did take a small walk, just to stretch my legs while I waited. I didn't park directly in front of Bianca's house because I was worried she wouldn't answer her door if she spotted my car out there."

I said, "You told Lieutenant Morrow that you'd planned on meeting with Bianca regarding family research. Something she'd discovered pertaining to your family. That she'd wanted to see you and share it. But it sounds instead like Bianca didn't want to meet with you at all."

Eleanor gave me a look that was dripping with dislike. "You're right, Bianca didn't have any research to share with me, although it was a plausible excuse for running by. I didn't want the police to misinterpret the situation."

"So, in actuality, you'd come by Bianca's house to confront her."

"Not *confront* her, simply reason with her," snapped Eleanor. "Anyway, when I came back around the block after my walk, I saw Sierra leaving. She was looking rather suspicious, to my way of thinking. Looking around her furtively as she left."

"You thought she looked suspicious at the time? Or after you found out Bianca was dead?" I asked.

Eleanor said in impatiently, "Afterwards, of course. I didn't think anything about it at the time. Just thought the young woman was behaving oddly. But then, so many young women do."

She gave me an imperious look as if she might classify me the same way.

"Did you say anything to the police about Sierra's manner?" I asked.

"No, I did not. I was worried that the police, not being the brightest of people, might consider *me* a suspect, simply because I'd been on the scene."

I considered this. "Did you go inside?"

Eleanor froze. "What do you mean?"

"Well, your entire purpose for being in the neighborhood was to speak with Bianca, right? You took a walk and noticed Sierra leaving. There was no longer any reason to wait to ring Bianca's doorbell. Did you go up to the house, ring the bell, get no answer, then walk inside?"

Eleanor had gone pale under her light tan. "Why would you think I would?"

"Because that's what I did. Bianca and I were supposed to have a meeting. I walked in when I didn't get an answer to my knocks or doorbell rings." I paused. "I think you did, too."

Eleanor took a deep breath. "I might have done that. I might have seen Bianca lying on the floor."

I said, "If you were like me, you went up to check for a pulse."

Eleanor nodded. "I did. I wasn't fond of Bianca Donovan, but I certainly didn't wish her ill. I didn't find a pulse. That's when I decided I should get out of there before the police completely misconstrued the situation."

I said, "You ended up being a suspect anyway, though, because of the nature of your relationship with Bianca."

Eleanor said haughtily, "There was no *relationship*. There was simply Bianca being extremely pushy and me trying to protect a family legacy and its property. Period. Who cared about the historic stuff Bianca uncovered? It wasn't important enough to prevent our family the use of our land. The land has been in the Johnson family for generations."

"My understanding is that you're wanting to sell some of that property?"

Eleanor stiffened. "It's our right. After all, it's our land. It's a desirably-located property. The fact that Bianca wanted to prevent us from tapping into a potential income source was very frustrating."

I said, "I'm surprised that, considering you were already a suspect, you didn't tell the police about Sierra's suspicious actions when you were there to see Bianca the morning she died."

"I just want this whole thing to go away. As far as I knew, Sierra arrived, saw that Bianca was already dead, and hurried away, the same as I did. Maybe Sierra simply didn't want to appear to be a suspect." Eleanor gave an impatient huff of a sigh. "Plus, I don't want to spend a bunch of my waking hours thinking or dealing with these things. This entire investigation has been very damaging to the family's reputation. I certainly don't want there to be a stain on our family name or my son's heritage. It's personally been very stressful for me."

"I'm sure it has been," I murmured.

Eleanor gave me a suspicious look, as if thinking I was being sarcastic. "I haven't been able to sleep. It's had a tremendous impact on the family." She gave a short laugh. "All I've ever wanted is to be part of a family."

"You're not close to your side of the family?"

Eleanor gave a short laugh. "There *is* no my side of the family. I grew up in foster care." She straightened. "When I was welcomed into the Johnson family, it's all I ever wanted. It's been such a blessing to be part of their clan."

"It sounds like they've been wonderful to you."

"Yes," said Eleanor. "And I don't want to pay back their kindness by dragging their name through the mud." She paused. "The police are looking in completely the wrong direction."

"The last time we spoke, you mentioned Daniel and Nolan were likely suspects. Is that still what you think?"

Eleanor sighed again. "I don't know what to think. This whole investigation has turned me topsy-turvy. But yes, if I have to pick two people who have significant reason to have murdered Bianca, I'd say those men would be at the top of my list. Daniel and Bianca would scrap all the time. And that Nolan."

Grayson gave Eleanor a charming smile, and I saw her warm to him. "I was wondering," said Grayson, "if you could explain the whole Nolan-Bianca situation. As an outsider, all I can see is they were both archaeologists. Since you follow history and archeology so closely, could you help fill me in?"

Eleanor was delighted to, clearly happy at being an expert in the situation. "Of course I will. First off, Nolan isn't an archaeologist at all. He's a CPA."

We knew this, but managed to look surprised since she expected it.

Eleanor continued, "Nolan is an *amateur* archaeologist. I'm not saying that he hasn't put a lot of time and effort into learning everything he can about archaeology. He and I have had some very interesting conversations about my family history and archeological information on the estate. Nolan did some digging for me in the South Carolina history room at the library, which was very helpful."

Grayson said slowly, "I'm guessing Bianca might not have seen Nolan as a full-fledged archeologist."

"Not a bit. That young woman was quite full of herself, in my opinion. Naturally, she did have a lot of degrees in the subject, which Nolan didn't have. But she didn't have to give him such a hard time."

Grayson tilted his head to one side. "What sort of hard time?"

Eleanor settled into her story with a look of satisfaction. "Well, I suppose the worst was several years ago. Bianca was giving a lecture at a prestigious archeological conference right here in Charleston. I attended, of course. In fact, I was one of the lecturers." Eleanor's expression was proud.

"That's wonderful," said Grayson. "What did you speak about?"

"Learning about and nurturing your family history for future generations. It was well-attended and people told me afterwards how very helpful it was."

"I'm sure it must have been," said Grayson.

Eleanor beamed at him. "Anyway, Bianca was talking about the importance of preserving historical sites and artifacts. I always thought Bianca's lectures were rather dry, but I wanted to attend that one since I figured she might mention my family's historic property."

"Did she?"

"No, she didn't, but she looked meaningfully at me several times during her presentation. Then, during the question-and-answer session that followed, Bianca was asked about an archeological find that had recently been discovered by a local enthusiast." Eleanor paused for dramatic effect. "That enthusiast was Nolan Harper, who was in attendance."

"What was Bianca's response?" asked Grayson.

"Gracious, she was so very abrasive. I suppose she considered herself straightforward, but she said very hurtful things. She criticized Nolan's find as amateurish, lacking proper archaeological methodology, and potentially damaging to the historical context of the site." Eleanor shook her head. "Poor Nolan. He kept sinking lower and lower into his chair. And he'd been so excited when the audience member asked about his find."

"Do you think Bianca really felt that way?" I asked. "Or was she just envious that Nolan had this major find?"

"Maybe a little bit of both," said Eleanor with a shrug. "She was quite passionate about archaeology, of course, and I suppose very unforgiving with mistakes, or perceived mistakes. The problem was that she made these remarks in front of a large audience, including very influential figures in the archaeological community. And the media, of course."

"Poor Nolan," said Grayson in a sympathetic voice.

Eleanor nodded. "Yes, it was quite awful. Bianca's comments were not only critical, but also dismissive. Bianca used quite strong language to convey her disapproval. The incident was covered by local news outlets. Nolan had invested significant time and resources in his discovery, and he felt totally discredited by Bianca."

"How did the local archaeological community view it?" I asked. "Did they try to pretend it didn't happen?"

"That proved very difficult to do with the news coverage," said Eleanor, pursing her lips. "The next conversation I had with Nolan afterwards was quite sad. He felt his standing in the community was tarnished. Nolan depended on private funding from individuals for projects, and those dried up for a while. It all left him with a deep-seated grudge against Bianca."

"That's obviously why you believe he might have murdered Bianca," said Grayson.

"That sounds dreadful when you put it that way," said Eleanor with a laugh. "But I suppose so. He was humiliated, you see. And I don't think Nolan is the type of person who takes that readily. He wanted to prove Bianca wrong in terms of her professional opinion of him. And he also deeply resented her. I can't see Nolan spearheading a planned attack on Bianca. But I could certainly see him lashing out at Bianca during a private conversation. He wanted to settle a score, you see. And her death did help eliminate a barrier to his own archaeological pursuits. He could continue on with his activities without Bianca's disapproval."

I glanced over at Grayson, and he nodded. "We should let you get back to your reading. Good seeing you, Eleanor," said Grayson in that winning way he had. "I knew you'd be full of information."

She looked pleased. "Well, I do spend a lot of my time researching and dealing with people. I guess those are skills that have served me well."

Chapter Twenty-One

We left Eleanor to her researching. "Still want to read the periodicals?" asked Grayson.

I said, "You know, I think I'm good right now. My mind is spinning so much that I'm not sure I'd be able to settle down to read magazines."

"Anywhere else you want to go or do? I know Holly's probably still on work calls, right?"

"It sounded that way," I said. I hesitated. Part of me just wanted to head back to Holly's house and read *South of Broad* for a while, with Fitz curled next to me. But if I couldn't focus on magazines, a book would surely be beyond me. "How about if we go by a coffeeshop or something? I could use a caffeine lift. And maybe a small bite to eat. I didn't really have anything at the funeral reception."

Grayson snapped his fingers. "You're right. We should be hungry. Let's hit a diner, though, instead of a coffeeshop. We need more food than just muffins or pastries."

So we headed for a diner that wasn't too far from Holly's place. Judging from the crowd indoors, it looked like it might be a good spot. I thought we might have to wait to be seated, but a couple left just as we were walking in. The diner had checkerboard floors in black and white, vinyl booths and barstools, and a glass display case showcasing their pies for the day.

A waitress with a ponytail and lots of eye makeup walked us to the table, called us honey, and gave us laminated menus. Just being in the diner was making my stomach growl with the smell of sizzling bacon, frying chicken, and freshly brewed coffee. We ordered sweet teas and an appetizer of fried green tomatoes to get started, then Grayson ordered a country fried steak, which arrived smothered in creamy gravy, served with buttery mashed potatoes and green beans. I chose a catfish po'boy which was served on a hoagie roll with lettuce, tomato, and remoulade sauce. We both got banana puddings for dessert.

We were chatting in-between bites of our food when a man stopped at our table. When I looked up, I was surprised to see Daniel there. He wasn't looking very good. His eyes were bloodshot, he hadn't shaved, and he looked as if he'd slept in his clothes the night before.

"Have you two seen Holly?" he asked brusquely.

"Yes. She's working back at the house. Having a busy day," I said.

Daniel looked only slightly relieved by this information. "So she's okay."

"She's fine." I was curter than I'd intended, but I'd had about enough of Daniel, and it seemed Holly had, too.

"The funny thing is, she's not answering my texts. Then I went by earlier and rang the doorbell, and she didn't come to the door." Daniel didn't seem as cocky as he had before. He was peering at my face searchingly.

"That's something you and Holly are going to have to discuss between the two of you," I said.

"So she's deliberately avoiding me."

"I can't speak to Holly's frame of mind. Like I said, she's very busy." I wasn't about to mention that Holly had found all of Daniel's appointments with Sierra on his calendar. That it seemed he was a lot more acquainted with her than he'd let on. And had been lying to the police and everyone else about that acquaintance.

Daniel rubbed his head absently. "I just don't know what's going on. I know you guys left the gallery early last night. I tried to call Holly after I left, but she didn't pick up then, either."

I shrugged. "She wanted to have an early night. She probably muted her phone so she could sleep." I wasn't going to give him anything.

Daniel sighed and sat down in one of the seats at our table. Grayson and I shared a look.

Daniel said, "I'm somehow getting the feeling Holly doesn't trust me. She wasn't like that before these murders happened. But now it's like she's lost faith in me or something. And I don't think she trusts me with other women. And maybe she thinks I'm a killer on top of it all. I can't figure out what's going on."

I said, "We're all just interested in finding out the truth, that's all. We want the police to figure out who did this and put him or her away."

"The truth is I had nothing to do with either of those deaths. Not Bianca's and not Sierra's. I didn't even know Sierra—why would I kill her?"

Daniel picked up on the quick glance Grayson and I shared. "What?" Daniel demanded. "You think I'm not telling the truth?"

Grayson decided to spill the beans. "Look, man, we realize now that you did know Sierra. In fact, you saw her quite a lot. So maybe that's one reason Holly isn't believing everything that comes out of your mouth."

Daniel looked surprised, then worried. "What do you mean you 'know' that?"

"Your calendar? The one you synched with Holly's last night? It had Sierra's name plastered all over it."

Now Daniel looked panicky. "Hey, whatever conclusions you've all drawn on that are totally wrong. I wasn't cheating on Holly."

"Maybe not," I said crisply, "but you definitely lied to her. And to the police, as well. You knew Sierra, even if she was just the person who gave you massages."

"You can't tell the police about that. They'll misunderstand everything. You know how they are—they just want to solve the case and move on to the next one. They'll be like a dog with a bone if they find out I knew Sierra. And I didn't do it. You'd just be wasting the cops' time."

Grayson said in a reasonable voice, "You've got to see how it looks."

"I do," Daniel's voice grew louder. He looked around quickly to make sure no one was listening in, but the diner was still bustling with customers, none of whom seemed at all interested in our conversation. "I tell you who did it. That other archaeologist guy. He's got to be the one who did it."

"What makes you think that?" I asked skeptically.

Daniel snorted. "Because Bianca complained about him all the time."

"Nolan said there was lots of mutual respect between them," I said.

"No way! Not at all. *Maybe* Nolan respected Bianca, but he sure didn't like her. And Bianca couldn't stand Nolan *and* had no respect for him. As far as Bianca was concerned, Nolan was like a loose cannon on those digs. Way too impatient to dig stuff up without taking the proper precautions and protocols into account."

"How do you know that?" asked Grayson.

"Because Bianca and I dated forever, remember? And she was always complaining about Nolan and his temper." Daniel wagged his finger, a thought occurring to him. "Plus, Nolan knew Sierra, too. They used to date each other. See? He's obviously the guy the police are looking for. Not me."

Before Grayson or I could say anything else, Daniel leaned in. "Tell Holly to pick up her phone. I really want to talk to her. She's gotten it all wrong."

We watched as he walked out of the diner.

Grayson said slowly, "That guy."

"I know. I'll let Holly know we ran into him, of course, but I really don't want her to make up with Daniel. Even if he's not a murderer, he just doesn't seem like someone to be in a long-term relationship with."

"Exactly. Although she's probably going to need to talk to Daniel at some point. At least to end the engagement." Grayson took a sip of his sweet tea. "Let's run through the whole thing again. I feel like everybody could have murdered Bianca and Sierra."

"That's the problem—they definitely could. So first, we have Daniel."

Grayson said, "Yeah, let's examine him first since he's the one I like the least. If he got locked up for murder, it sure would be easier for Holly to ditch him."

"I think she's going to find it easy to ditch him, regardless. So from what we can tell, Daniel and Bianca were still very much in touch. We've heard from Sierra that they were having an on-again-off-again relationship . . . that maybe Daniel and Bianca were still sort of seeing each other, even though Daniel was engaged. Everyone else has said that they ran into each other professionally, especially when they were arguing for government money to be allocated to their pet projects."

Grayson nodded. "And either way, it sounds like they weren't getting along. That they were publicly arguing all the time. And, if they were arguing in public, could it have gotten more heated in private?"

"It sounds that way. Plus, Daniel covered up the fact that he knew and spent time with Sierra Barnett. He'd told Holly and the police that he wasn't acquainted with her. But he had all those dates in his calendar with Sierra. We don't know if those were personal or professional."

Grayson said, "I guess we're thinking Daniel killed Sierra because she knew he'd murdered Bianca?"

I nodded. "If he did kill her. He didn't care anything about beach renourishment, so it most likely would have been that Sierra had evidence against him. So that's Daniel."

"Who also doesn't have a good alibi for either murder," said Grayson. "Who's next?"

"Nolan appears to have plenty of motive. Eleanor Johnson was kind enough to elaborate on that a little. It sounds like Bianca not only thought very little of Nolan's amateur archaeology, she also put him down in a public forum with a lot of important people in the field in attendance. And from what we've heard from others, Bianca was often dismissive of Nolan in other instances, too."

Grayson frowned. "So Nolan could have gone over to Bianca's house on Saturday morning, when he was off work. Maybe he wanted to have a word with her about her treatment of him."

I shrugged. "Or maybe he wanted to discuss some new find he'd discovered. Bianca could have reacted in that same dismissive way and it was one time too often for him. Nolan could have lost it and strangled Bianca."

"And again, Sierra, who'd come to the house to give Bianca a massage, could have witnessed Nolan leaving the house and later confronted him about it."

I nodded. "Which would have meant he'd want to eliminate Sierra as a witness. Then we have the developer, Cooper Thornton."

"He's a guy who has a lot on the line," said Grayson. "That hotel development of his sounds like a huge project. He didn't want that to be scrapped for lack of sand."

"Competition for sand is definitely a big deal here. The turtles need it. I was reading that beach-nesting birds also rely on it. Tourists need it, too. Erosion has gotten to be a big issue, and fixing it is expensive."

Grayson said, "So Cooper naturally wasn't very happy that Bianca was possibly shutting down his development to protect the Stone Fleet. He might have gone over to have a conversation with Bianca about supporting beach renourishment and then things got out of hand. Just like the possible scenario between Nolan and Bianca. Sierra might have seen *Cooper* coming out of Bianca's house, and Cooper decided to get rid of her to keep her from talking."

"Right. He also doesn't come off as totally sincere to me. It feels like he talks a good game about the development being important for jobs and tourism, but I get the impression the most important thing to Cooper is his bank account."

Grayson said, "Who else do we have?"

"Eleanor Johnson. She may not seem like the most likely person to strangle Bianca, but she's in excellent shape, strong, and very passionate about her family's history."

"And her family's property," said Grayson. "I remember Cooper telling us that Eleanor had reached out to him wanting to sell a piece of their property for development."

"Which makes sense, if the family has property instead of liquid assets. It sounded like the Johnsons might be in some financial difficulty."

"But that pesky Bianca managed to find historically significant artifacts on the Johnson estate," said Grayson. "Eleanor must have been furious about that."

"She definitely seems very invested in both keeping the family's good reputation and keeping them financially solvent," I said.

Grayson fished some money out of his wallet for the meals and the tip. "Where do we go from here?"

I sighed. "I guess we should head back to Holly's house. After she's done with her meetings, we should let her know we ran into Daniel."

"If Daniel isn't camping out in front of her house. He seemed really shaken up that Holly wasn't responding to him."

I made a face. "Probably because he's used to Holly jumping whenever he wants something. Which isn't like Holly at all. She has so much love to give. I just don't want her wasting it on the wrong person."

When we got back, we were relieved to see that Daniel wasn't lurking outside Holly's house. We walked inside the house and were greeted ecstatically by Murphy. Fitz gave us a more restrained but still very affectionate greeting. Then the two animals lay next to each other in a sunbeam on the kitchen floor. I grabbed my *South of Broad* book and Grayson picked up the World War II book he was reading.

About thirty minutes after we got back, Holly got off her meeting. She looked tired, but composed. "Did your meetings go okay?" I asked.

Holly nodded. "They did. I just wish there were fewer of them. Sometimes I swear people just like to hear themselves talk." She stretched her arms over her head. Then she looked at us. "Why do you both have those funny expressions on your faces?"

I said, "We ran into Daniel when we went to a diner for lunch."

"Did you lose your appetite? I would have." She sighed. "I finally had to mute my phone because he was calling and texting so much. I know I've got to talk to him, but between Bianca's funeral and all these meetings, I haven't figured out what I'm going to say. I'm definitely ending our engagement, though. I can't spend my life with somebody I don't trust." She gave a wry smile. "I bet my parents will throw a party in celebration."

I felt a wave of relief and thought that *I* might throw a party. And I'm a major introvert. I gave Holly a hug. "I'm sorry. I know that was a hard decision to reach."

She hugged me back. "Thanks, Ann. I'm so glad you guys were here. And I'm sorry you were here, too. This wasn't exactly what you signed up for when you came down here. Murder and broken engagements." Holly paused. "What do you make of all this, Grayson?"

He said staunchly, "That you're making the right decision. I kept getting the feeling Daniel had a wandering eye."

"That's a nice way of putting it." Holly's voice was rueful. "So what did Daniel say when you saw him? Don't worry—it's not going to change my decision."

I said, "He was explaining how he was misunderstood. That he had nothing to do with the murders at all. He asked us to tell you to call him. I half-thought he was going to be lurking somewhere on the grounds, waiting for you to leave so he could talk to you."

Holly shook her head. "That wouldn't have gone well. I'm glad he didn't try that. How did he look?"

Grayson said, "Actually, he looked pretty bad. Bloodshot eyes, clothes he probably slept in."

"Good," said Holly fiercely. "He's messed with my emotions too much for me to care about his." She rubbed her face. "The longer this goes on, though, the worst it's going to get. I'm going to go see him in person. I might as well get it over with." She pulled the ring off her finger.

"Do you want me to go with you?" I asked. "Even if I just stay in the car?"

Holly shook her head. "Daniel's not dangerous." Then she gave a short laugh. "Unless he murdered Bianca and Sierra, of course."

"Maybe *I* should wait in the car," said Grayson grimly.

Holly stood up. "Why don't we all go? This is going to be short and sweet. Having y'all in the car will be the perfect excuse for me to leave instead of having to go through a post-mortem of our entire relationship. Then we'll do something fun together."

"Wine?" I asked, thinking of Holly's proclivity for wine-drinking the last few days.

"Even better," she said. "Ice cream."

Holly was as good as her word. Grayson and I waited in her car. She went inside Daniel's apartment, but only for about ten minutes. When she left, she was no longer carrying the ring. Her expression was resolved, but tinged with sadness.

"Ice cream!" she said.

Chapter Twenty-Two

We didn't ask how it had all gone, and Holly seemed glad not to talk about it. No matter how upset you are at someone, it couldn't be easy to end a relationship that was as serious as theirs was.

A few minutes later, we were walking into an old-fashioned ice cream parlor called Sweet Scoops. Holly treated herself to triple chocolate fudge and cookies and cream in a waffle cone. Grayson skipped the chocolate route altogether and picked a salted caramel swirl with a scoop of butter pecan in a cup. I was the boring member of the group and went with vanilla. I figured life had been complicated enough already, and having something simple was calling to me.

After our ice cream, we headed back to Holly's house. She was quieter than she'd been at the ice cream parlor. When we walked inside, she and Murphy headed to the backyard to hang out for a while. Holly said she was going to call her parents and give them the news. I hoped Holly's mom and dad managed to temper their relief, for Holly's sake. Grayson and I gave Holly some space by heading to the beach for a while. It was a great way to do nothing, which was something I sorely needed.

Grayson and I lay on the sand, feeling the late-day sun on us. Grayson had a great playlist, which he played on his phone. We heard the waves in the background, which lulled us both to sleep for a while.

Maybe it was because of the nap I'd taken, or maybe it was the fact that we all turned in early after Grayson and I returned from the beach. But I found myself up early the next morning—too early to even make breakfast for the others. I made myself some eggs with toast, then decided it might be good for my stress levels to take a jog. Grayson had gotten us both a gym membership back in Whitby, and we'd been good to go over there at least three times a week. I knew vacations were for taking breaks from the ordinary, but I was missing my workouts a little.

I slipped upstairs and changed into shorts and a tee shirt. I wrote a note to the others, letting them know where I'd gone. I also pulled up my safety app on my phone, which I always used whenever I exercised alone. I stretched for a few minutes, then set out with Holly's extra key in my pocket.

It was the perfect time to go for a jog. The humidity was low, and there was a brisk breeze, keeping the air even cooler. It was early enough that the rush hour traffic hadn't started up yet, helping keep the roads clear for me. I set out at a steady pace. The folks I saw along the way were letting their dogs out and setting out their trashcans for collection, and getting started with their days.

I was turning a corner when I nearly ran into someone jogging from the other side. After recovering from the surprise of nearly plowing into someone, we both recognized each other. It was Cooper Thornton. He was wearing what looked to be designer jogging duds, as opposed to my low-key outfit. He also wasn't nearly as sweaty as I was.

"Sorry," I said, still catching my breath. "I wasn't watching where I was going."

Cooper gave me that cheerful salesman smile. "Oh, it was my fault. My head was a million miles away." He pointed at himself. "I thought if I exercised more that I might keep up better with Elana on the dance floor."

"I've already heard you ditched her on the dance floor to head back home early Monday night," I said with a smile. I saw an odd expression flash across his face before he returned to his genial grin.

"Well, I guess that's what happens when you date somebody who's a lot younger than you are," he said wryly. "Of course, you seem to have been smarter and are going out with someone your own age."

I smiled back at him. "It just sort of happened that way. I guess we really can't change the way we meet someone, regardless of their age." I paused. "I'm glad I ran into you, actually."

"No pun intended," said Cooper with a merry look in his eyes.

"Right. I wanted to ask you about the money you're planning on giving in Sierra's memory. To the turtle team. I'd like to give a small amount, too. I don't have your kind of budget, but I've really liked everything I've heard about the turtle team."

Cooper looked pleased. "It's a great cause. I've got a number of philanthropic causes, if you'd like to have other opportunities to give. I fund scholarships, for example, that help pay for after-school programs and educational initiatives designed to support students in underserved communities. And, of course, I like giving to the local arts programs, including the one Daniel is affiliated with. I know Holly and Daniel will end up being major elements in promoting the arts in Charleston."

I decided not to say anything about Holly and Daniel's breakup. If Charleston were like any other Southern town, the word would already be spreading.

"Those do sound like great opportunities for giving," I said. "But I'd better be smart with my budget and start small."

Cooper said, "You can give to the group online. I've got a link earmarked for the turtle team on their website and put in a blurb about Sierra and her dedication to the cause. I've been thinking that they could bring in more tourism with different types of turtle walks. At Edisto Beach State Park, you can take a ranger-guided *nighttime* beach walk to witness a loggerhead nesting or the hatchlings staggering off to the ocean. And Huntington Beach and Hunting Island State Parks also offer educational programs on sea turtles during the summer season. Isle of Palms should do more to raise awareness . . . money, too."

"They did a great job with the walk I was on," I mentioned, feeling a little defensive for poor Sierra.

"Oh, I'm sure they did. They could just *expand* on what they're already doing, you know? I thought Sierra did such a great job with her patrols. She was always out there every Tuesday morning during the season. I often saw her there when I was walking my dog, Bowser."

I froze. Cooper had said he'd never met Sierra, aside from a moment at a town hall meeting. I tried to control my features.

"Yes, she seemed really devoted to it. Well, it was good seeing you, Cooper. I'd better get on with my jog before it starts getting really hot out there."

I could feel Cooper's narrowed eyes on my back and set off at a faster pace than I had before. Plus, I'd turned around to head back to Holly's house. I wanted to tell the lieutenant what Cooper had said. I just hoped Cooper wasn't suspicious—that I hadn't given myself away. It also occurred to me that Cooper had shown an immediate reaction when I basically told him his alibi for Sierra's death was no good—that he hadn't been out late the night before at all.

But a minute later, I realized he was definitely suspicious. That's when I heard feet pounding the pavement behind me and felt myself shoved right into a narrow alley between townhomes.

Chapter Twenty-Three

"You're not going anywhere," said Cooper in a harsh tone. "You did it," I said. I wanted to buy time. Had anyone seen him shove me back here? "You killed Sierra. You told me you didn't know her. Then you suddenly have an intimate knowledge of her schedule?" I huffed out a short laugh. "But you didn't kill Bianca, did you? You had Sierra do your dirty work for you."

"You think you're so smart, don't you?" Cooper's face had transformed into something ruthless.

I took a shaky breath. "You knew Sierra. Maybe you were one of her clients. Maybe you were in a relationship with her. You convinced her Bianca was never going to let the Stone Fleet go. That there wouldn't be sand for the turtles. And you knew Bianca was one of Sierra's clients. It would be easy for a massage therapist to strangle someone."

"Just shut your mouth," hissed Cooper. "You don't know what you're talking about."

"I think I do," I said, still stalling. Hoping I could catch my breath and get another burst of energy so I could get away. "The problem was that Sierra started feeling bad about what she'd done, didn't she? I spoke with a woman who said she hadn't been the same since Bianca's death. Sierra told her that she'd screwed up. Sierra seemed to feel guilty. Perhaps she wanted to go to the police. And the problem with that was that she was going to throw you under the bus, too. So you had to get rid of her."

Cooper lunged for me, which was when I set off the self-protection app on my phone. Its blaring was ear-piercing and a tremendous relief, all at the same time. Cooper snarled at me, his pleasant features twisted. I regained my balance from the shove and drove the heel of my palm right into Cooper's nose. He yelled, blood spurting from his face as I broke free from his grip and started running in earnest.

I heard Cooper coming up behind me again as I ran. But now, there were people coming outside, drawn by the screeching alarm of my app and my own screams for help.

"I'm calling the cops," shouted one woman, and I nodded.

I didn't know what Cooper's endgame was at this point. Maybe he was just so furious at me and so desperate that he wasn't really thinking about the fact that he was tearing after me, clearly wanting to assault me with a bunch of witnesses looking on.

Some tiny bit of rationality must have entered his brain because he finally dropped back with a curse, heading off in the other direction. A cop must have been close by because there was a chirp of a siren, then an oscillating wail as neighbors pointed in the direction Cooper had run in. I was completely spent. I dropped to the curb, panting. I'd never been much for sprinting and the total terror I felt didn't help.

A woman from a nearby house brought me water and made angry noises about awful men while I drank it.

"Can I call anybody for you, love?" she asked me.

I realized I probably needed to call Lieutenant Morrow. But my arms and legs felt like jelly. "Could you call a particular police officer?"

"Somebody you know, love?" she asked. "Of course I will."

I gave her the number off my phone and she cleared her throat many times while dialing it. I could hear Morrow's answer, which was right when the woman started clucking at him. "You should come here! A man tried to kill her! Right in front of all of us."

Morrow now sounded both confused and focused all at once. "Who did?"

The woman put the phone on speaker. I said, still breathless. "It's Ann. Ann Beckett. Cooper Thornton is the murderer."

"Where are you?" asked Morrow, his voice steely.

I looked helplessly at the woman. I wasn't sure what street I was on. She crisply filled him in, then spat out, "Hurry! This poor girl has had the fright of her life! Imagine men like that out on the streets!" Then she hung up.

To his credit, Morrow was indeed there in what felt like a mere five minutes. He gave me a cursory look when he got out of his car. "You're okay?" he asked.

I nodded. "A lot better than Bianca and Sierra, that's for sure."

"Let's get you out of here. Back to your friend's house. Holly?"

I nodded again, and Morrow gave me a lift to her house. He accompanied me inside, where he immediately got a phone call. Morrow listened for a few moments, responded in monosyllabic words, then hung up. "They got him."

It was still early in the morning. Grayson, hearing a strange voice, hurried downstairs, still wiping sleep from his eyes. Holly came in from her office, eyes wide. "What's going on?" she asked.

Grayson was already wrapping his arms around me. "Are you okay?"

I nodded, biting my lip to keep the tears at bay. "I'm okay. I went for a jog before it started getting hot. I ran into Cooper Thornton."

"What did he do?" asked Grayson, eyes narrowing.

"If we can all take a seat?" asked Morrow. "I'd like to hear what Ann has to say, too."

We all sat down in the living room. I was relieved because I just wasn't sure my legs were going to support me anymore.

"Was Cooper Thornton following you?" asked Morrow.

I shook my head. "No. He was out jogging, too. We were both coming around a blind corner at the same time and almost collided. So we started talking."

Morrow was jotting down notes. "What was the topic of conversation?"

"Well, eventually, it was Sierra. Cooper had mentioned donating money to the turtle team in honor of Sierra. I said I'd like to make a small donation myself."

Morrow was watching me with his steady gaze. He gave a small nod, encouraging me to keep going. Somehow, my mouth was still dry, though, despite the glass of water the woman had given me earlier. Holly seemed to notice and leaped up to get me something to drink.

"Then Cooper started talking about all the other kinds of philanthropies he supported. But toward the end, he said how dedicated Sierra was. How she was always out on the beach every Tuesday." I shrugged. "But before, he'd said he didn't even know Sierra. So how did he know her schedule so well?"

Morrow said slowly, "And Cooper could tell that you noticed his slip."

"Oh yeah. I tried to cover up my expression, but I guess I didn't do a good job. He'd already shown a reaction earlier when I mentioned that I'd heard he hadn't been out late dancing Monday night."

Morrow looked confused. "Dancing?"

"Right. Cooper had told us he'd been out dancing with Elana. That he'd slept in Tuesday morning when Sierra was murdered. But Elana totally refuted that when I talked to her later. She said he came home early Monday night and always woke at five a.m. I guess between the two things, Cooper realized I knew he was the murderer."

Grayson looked grim as Morrow jotted down more notes.

"I made some excuse about needing to finish my jog, then I set off in the opposite direction that I'd been heading in when he and I almost ran into each other." Holly handed me a glass of iced tea, which I drank down thirstily.

Morrow waited for me to drink some more. "What happened then?"

"He cornered me and shoved me into an alley," I said, trying to be as straightforward as possible. I heard Grayson and Holly gasp, but I tried not to focus on my emotions at all. Not how scared and trapped I'd felt. I was proud that there wasn't a wobble in my voice when I continued. "I realized something else when I was in that alley. I don't think Cooper killed Bianca at all. I think he convinced Sierra to do his dirty work for him."

"What makes you think that?" asked Morrow in as level a voice as I was using.

"A couple of things. For one, Sierra was at Bianca's house that Saturday morning. Her car was there—it was spotted by a couple of people. Maybe Sierra thought taking her personal vehicle over to Bianca's place wouldn't be as noticeable as her work van. No one reported seeing a man at the house or Cooper's vehicle there. Plus, Cooper didn't seem at the time like someone who wanted to get his hands dirty."

Grayson gave an angry laugh. "That obviously changed."

"It did. I think he got increasingly desperate. Cooper started really getting worried that he was going to get caught and go to jail for this."

Morrow asked, "You think Cooper and Sierra were in a relationship with each other?"

"It's possible. It would have been one way of making her invested enough to get rid of Bianca. Or maybe he just convinced her that she would be the better choice to strangle Bianca. Obviously, when you're getting a massage, you're relaxed. Sometimes half-asleep. It would have been an easy way to attack someone. Plus, Bianca trusted Sierra, even though they were on opposite sides of the beach issue."

Morrow nodded, jotting down more notes. "Anything else?"

I said, "One of the turtle team members said on the beach that Sierra had been in a strange mood since Bianca's death. That she seemed disturbed and mentioned some sort of screw-up she'd made. Maybe Sierra was having second thoughts and feeling guilty about what she'd done. Maybe she was thinking about turning herself in and throwing Cooper under the bus, too. That would mean that Cooper would need to eliminate Sierra to keep himself from being exposed. Plus, Sierra had been lying to us all along. She said she'd slept in the morning Bianca died, but her silver car was in front of Bianca's house, spotted by several people. Plus, Sierra never mentioned that Bianca was a client of hers. She was downplaying any kind of personal connection."

"You mentioned these things to Cooper Thornton?" asked Morrow

"Some of them, yes. I was trying at that point to just keep talking and buy myself some time. I could tell that what I was saying was hitting home. He was furious. He was also mad at all the noise I was making. I'd been screaming the whole time I was running away from Cooper."

Morrow said, "And people were paying attention."

"Sure they were. It's a peaceful neighborhood here. If a woman is running down the street screaming, people are going to notice. Somebody told me they'd called the cops. Folks were outside, getting ready to head to work. And there's some maniac trying to attack a woman right there in their neighborhood."

Morrow gave a small smile. "The station told me Cooper was pretty beaten up. That he was having to get medical treatment for a broken nose."

Holly started clapping, and I gave a short laugh. "Well, that makes me feel good. I'd taken a self-defense class at the library some time ago. Our police chief put it on. I'm glad I could remember some moves from the class."

"Me, too," said Grayson darkly.

I continued, "So, I broke away from Cooper and was able to make it to a safe spot. A woman brought me water and also phoned the police. I heard sirens almost immediately." I shrugged. "You know the rest."

"And he's definitely been arrested?" demanded Holly, hands on her hips.

"That's correct," said Morrow. "He's also confessed." He looked back at me again. "Just to Sierra's murder. We should be able to corroborate that. Sierra did attempt to fight back. We believe we'll be able to match DNA found under her nails to Cooper Thornton."

"And he'll also be charged in Bianca's death, won't he?" I asked. "Even if he didn't kill her directly?"

"I'm imagining he'll likely be charged as an accessory to murder. Or, possibly, for conspiracy to commit murder," said Morrow. He stood up, closing his notebook. "I'm sorry you've had such a rough time in Charleston. I promise the city is a lot safer than it might appear. I hope you'll come back another time and see us at our best." For once, he gave a smile that softened his stern features.

"Oh, I will," I said. "Grayson and I love the beaches, the food, and Holly."

Holly gave us a rueful smile. "I'm glad to hear you're willing to risk a return visit."

Chapter Twenty-Four

The rest of the day, the three of us made a point to relax as much as possible. Holly took the afternoon off and we went to the beach, watching surfers at Folly navigate the waves. We all got a little too much sun, but enjoyed every minute, listening to Grayson's music, reading books, and laughing with each other. Holly seemed so much lighter, freer. I was glad to see the old Holly back, although I did sense some sadness below the surface.

The next morning, Grayson, Fitz, and I headed back to Whitby. Fitz napped in his carrier the whole way, and I was surprised to find that I did the same. I'd intended on taking a turn at the wheel on the way home. I woke up, startled, to find that we were just twenty-five miles from home.

I struggled to sit up, having slumped over in the passenger seat. "I meant to drive halfway."

Grayson gave me a cheerful smile. "Nope! When I saw how sacked out you were, I figured it would be smarter to let you sleep."

"True. Considering how tired I was, I might have been dangerous behind the wheel." I stretched and looked into the backseat. Fitz was stretching too, his mouth opening in an enormous yawn. "Looks like Fitz got in a good nap, too."

When we got back to my house, Grayson helped me unload my stuff and then gently brought Fitz inside. Fitz looked around the cottage with pleasure, happy to be home, and immediately rolled on his back in a sunbeam. Grayson and I chuckled at him, and I saw a corresponding feline smile on Fitz's face.

"You probably feel you need a vacation from your vacation," said Grayson. "Should you take tomorrow off from work?"

I shook my head. "I'm ready to take on all the library chaos. It'll seem a lot quieter than our Charleston trip."

Grayson suddenly looked a little shy. "It really was such a crazy trip. I kept looking for a good time to give you this, but there never seemed to be a good moment." He reached into a tote bag he'd slung on his shoulder and pulled out a rectangular box wrapped in tissue paper. He cleared his throat. "Holly helped me with a box and paper."

I'd never seen him look quite so uncertain. I reached gently for the box and unwrapped it. It was a Navajo squash blossom necklace with intricate silverwork and turquoise accents. I ran my hand over it. "It's beautiful."

"I know you don't wear a lot of jewelry," said Grayson hastily. "If it's not your style, I understand."

I smiled at him. "I don't wear a lot of jewelry because I don't *have* a lot of jewelry." I looked at the necklace again. "This looks vintage."

Grayson cleared his throat. "It is. I found it while I was clearing out my uncle's house when you and Holly were out. It used to be my great-great-grandmother's necklace—she'd gotten it from a trip to Sante Fe in the late 1800s. I got interested in it and found some old pictures and letters talking about it."

"But it's a family piece," I said slowly. "Wouldn't you like to hold onto it?"

He shook his head. "I'd love for you to have it. If you want, that is."

My smile widened, and I slipped the necklace over my head. "I'd be honored." I walked over to a mirror near my front door and admired the necklace. "It's beautiful," I said again.

"I looked the squash blossom necklaces up online," said Grayson quickly. I got the feeling he was trying to keep our conversation on the lighter side. I sort of understood, considering we'd just seen an engagement go completely sideways in the last week. I was glad we were taking things slowly.

Grayson continued, "The turquoise is considered a sacred stone by Native Americans. It's supposed to offer protection, healing, and positive energy. And the squash blossom symbolizes prosperity."

I reached out and pulled him in for a hug, followed by a long kiss. "I can use all of those things. Thank you, Grayson."

He hugged me back tightly. Then he smiled at me. "I'd better head back and unpack. Take it easy, okay?" He gave me a light kiss on the lips.

I nodded. Although what he was saying was casual, I could feel from the way he said it that he cherished me. And how much he cared. But I was also glad we were taking things slowly. There wasn't any need to jump into an engagement or marriage. I'd seen too many of those fall by the wayside. Right now, it was enough for us to be together.

Holly called a few minutes after Grayson left.

"Just wanted to make sure you got home okay," she said.

I said ruefully, "We did, although with no help from me. I ended up falling asleep and poor Grayson drove the whole way."

"You've got a good guy there, you know," said Holly in a wistful voice.

"I do know. And you're going to find one, too."

Holly said slowly, "After y'all left, I was feeling . . . oh, I don't know. Maybe a little bereft. I decided to go spend some money," she said with a short laugh.

"Retail therapy," I said in the tone of one who knew, although I didn't.

This made Holly laugh. "Like you'd ever go out and blow money to make yourself feel better."

I laughed too. "You know me too well. Maybe, if I *had* money to blow, that's what I'd do."

"Somehow, I doubt that. Anyway, I figured it would just make me feel worse to spend money on clothes, since I'd just condemned myself to being alone. So I went back to that used bookstore we went to with my mom."

A smile spread across my face as I remembered the young man with the wire-rimmed glasses. "Right. That was a nice guy who owned the shop. Bill?"

"Ben. Ben Carter. He asked me what kind of book I was looking for." Holly gave a short laugh. "You're not going to believe this, but I burst into tears."

"Hey, you've been through a lot the last week."

Holly said, "Ben was just so kind. I think that's what made me do it. I'm fine unless somebody tries to be kind to me. Anyway, I explained that I'd just broken up with my boyfriend."

I had the feeling that Ben was delighted to hear that, even if he'd probably wisely covered up that fact. "Knowing that, what books did he recommend for you?"

I could hear Holly grinning through the phone. "He's an expert, Ann. I mean, you are too, of course. Guess what he pulled out for me."

I considered the question. "Is it fiction or non-fiction?"

"Both!"

I said, "Okay, I'm not sure about the fiction, but I'm guessing the non-fiction might be *Eat, Pray, Love.*"

"Oh, you're good. Yes, that was one of the books."

"Well, that's a good one," I said. "Honestly, I could keep guessing all day on the fiction, so why don't you tell me."

"*Heartburn* by Nora Ephron."

I smiled. "I'm liking Ben Carter more and more."

"That's good, because he asked me if we could have coffee together sometime," said Holly.

"That Ben moves quickly. But then, he's got to know that someone like you isn't going to be available for long."

"Thanks, Ann," said Holly. "He gave me his number and told me to call him whenever I felt up to it. I thought about it, and I'm not going to wait for long. After all, the last thing I need to do is sit around and mope over Daniel Reynolds."

I spent the rest of the day unpacking and doing laundry. Then I knocked out the rest of my book on the sofa, curled up with Fitz.

The next morning, I was on the schedule to open the library. Even though it meant an early start, I was glad to do it. Mornings at the library, especially when no one else was there yet, were my favorite time of the day. Fitz, knowing the routine, happily walked back into his carrier, and I headed the short distance to work. The sun was peaking over the horizon, casting a soft glow on the town.

I parked the car and headed inside with Fitz in tow, locking the door behind me so early-bird patrons wouldn't follow me in. I let Fitz out of his carrier and he padded around, making a lap around the building, checking out the stacks and reading nooks before joining me at the circulation desk. I returned *South of Broad*, which I'd finished last night. I looked around the library, full of books waiting to be explored, worlds ready to be discovered, and stories to be told.

About the Author

Bestselling cozy mystery author Elizabeth Spann Craig is a library-loving, avid mystery reader. A pet-owning Southerner, her four series are full of cats, corgis, and cheese grits. The mother of two, she lives with her husband, a fun-loving corgi, and a couple of cute cats.

Sign up for Elizabeth's free newsletter to stay updated on releases:

https://bit.ly/2xZUXqO

This and That

I love hearing from my readers. You can find me on Facebook as Elizabeth Spann Craig Author, on Twitter as elizabeth-scraig, on my website at elizabethspanncraig.com, and by email at elizabethspanncraig@gmail.com.

Thanks so much for reading my book...I appreciate it. If you enjoyed the story, would you please leave a short review on the site where you purchased it? Just a few words would be great. Not only do I feel encouraged reading them, but they also help other readers discover my books. Thank you!

Did you know my books are available in print and ebook formats? Most of the Myrtle Clover series is available in audio and some of the Southern Quilting mysteries are. Find the audiobooks here: https://elizabethspanncraig.com/audio/

Please follow me on BookBub for my reading recommendations and release notifications.

I'd also like to thank some folks who helped me put this book together. Thanks to my cover designer, Karri Klawiter, for her awesome covers. Thanks to my editor, Judy Beatty for her help. Thanks to beta readers Amanda Arrieta, Rebecca Wahr, Cassie Kelley, and Dan Harris for all of their helpful suggestions and careful reading. Thanks to my ARC readers for helping to spread the word. Thanks, as always, to my family and readers.

Other Works by Elizabeth

Myrtle Clover Series in Order (be sure to look for the Myrtle series in audio, ebook, and print):

Pretty is as Pretty Dies
Progressive Dinner Deadly
A Dyeing Shame
A Body in the Backyard
Death at a Drop-In
A Body at Book Club
Death Pays a Visit
A Body at Bunco
Murder on Opening Night
Cruising for Murder
Cooking is Murder
A Body in the Trunk
Cleaning is Murder
Edit to Death
Hushed Up
A Body in the Attic
Murder on the Ballot
Death of a Suitor

A Dash of Murder

Death at a Diner

A Myrtle Clover Christmas

Murder at a Yard Sale

Doom and Bloom

A Toast to Murder

Mystery Loves Company (2025)

THE VILLAGE LIBRARY Mysteries in Order:

Checked Out

Overdue

Borrowed Time

Hush-Hush

Where There's a Will

Frictional Characters

Spine Tingling

A Novel Idea

End of Story

Booked Up

Out of Circulation

Shelf Life (2025)

The Sunset Ridge Mysteries in Order

The Type-A Guide to Solving Murder

The Type-A Guide to Dinner Parties (2025)

Southern Quilting Mysteries in Order:

Quilt or Innocence

Knot What it Seams

Quilt Trip
Shear Trouble
Tying the Knot
Patch of Trouble
Fall to Pieces
Rest in Pieces
On Pins and Needles
Fit to be Tied
Embroidering the Truth
Knot a Clue
Quilt-Ridden
Needled to Death
A Notion to Murder
Crosspatch
Behind the Seams
Quilt Complex
A Southern Quilting Cozy Christmas (Oct. 2024)

MEMPHIS BARBEQUE MYSTERIES in Order (Written as Riley Adams):
Delicious and Suspicious
Finger Lickin' Dead
Hickory Smoked Homicide
Rubbed Out
And a standalone "cozy zombie" novel: Race to Refuge, written as Liz Craig

Made in United States
North Haven, CT
14 June 2024

53615634R00124